MARIQUITA
-revisited

"*Mariquita* is an important novel about the tragedy of World War II in Japanese-occupied Guam. May you enjoy, as I did, its unique Chamorro interpretation of love and loss in a place of unending war."

—**KEITH L. CAMACHO**, Ph.D., associate professor of Asian American Studies, University of California, Los Angeles

"Through Chris Perez Howard's researching and writing, he was seeking to rediscover his mother and her life that was tragically cut short by war. In *Mariquita*, we see an attempt to find fullness, to give that greatest generation of ours a story it is due. With each passing year, more of the war survivor generation pass on. The task of telling the stories of our elders and carrying forward their wisdom has already fallen to us. *Mariquita* remains an important text for those seeking to retell the stories of our elders in a form worthy of their struggle, their sacrifice and their survival."

—**MICHAEL LUJAN BEVACQUA**, Ph.D., historian, writer and professor, University of Guam

"*Mariquita* was the first novel I found that depicted us as a people. When I read *Mariquita* for the first time, I was a junior in high school and I found it in a series of articles in the Sunday edition of the *Guam Tribune* that I was reading in the MARC Library. I remember waiting impatiently for the next segment of the story because I wanted to know more about her and more about the Guam she lived in. Through her experiences, I became immersed in the Guam of our parents, grandparents, and ancestors. Through her eyes, I could see the importance of family, culture and tradition – even as society was changing. Through her heart, I felt more deeply the powerful love that Guam's families feel for each other. Mariquita taught me about the importance of history because her story showed me how history is made up of generations and generations of our experiences."

—**MONIQUE CARRIVEAU STORIE**, Ph.D., dean, University Libraries, University of Guam

"In his biographical novel *Mariquita*, Chris Perez Howard takes us on a journey of reconnection with his mother as well as his cultural heritage. The accessibility of the narrative and its revealing of the horrors of war make it an important contribution to the larger collection of documented World War II oral history and literature."

—**LEIANA SAN AGUSTIN NAHOLOWA'A**, instructor, Women and Gender Studies, University of Guam

MARIQUITA

-revisited

Chris Perez Howard

Published by Taiguini Books, University of Guam Press
Richard Flores Taitano Micronesian Area Research Center

UOG Station
303 University Drive
Mangilao, Guam 96913
(671) 735-2154
www.uog.edu/uogpress

Edited by Victoria-Lola Leon Guerrero
Cover and Interior Design by Jess Merrill

ISBN 978-1-935198-34-5

In honor of my mother

Marquita

Contents

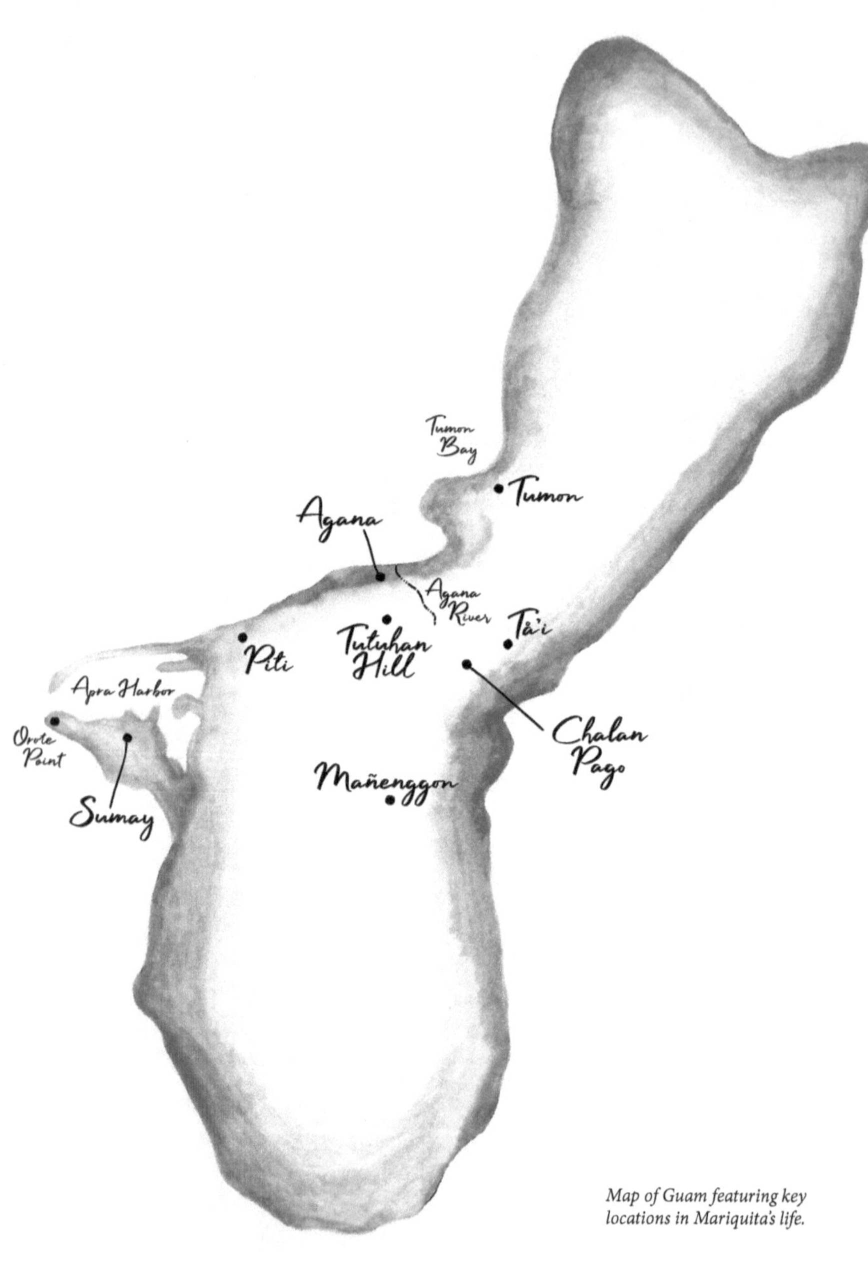

Map of Guam featuring key locations in Mariquita's life.

Preface

I WAS BORN ON Guam in 1940 but left when I was five years old. Aside from a two-year stay from 1949-1951, I lived primarily in the United States. In 1979, I returned after twenty-seven years away and saw a Guam I did not know.

Prior to my return, I had been living in St. Thomas in the U.S. Virgin Islands. From there, I contacted my Uncle Felix who was living in California and told him that I was going to Guam and asked him to contact a family member to meet me at the airport and help me settle in. When I arrived at the airport in Guam, I was surprised to see a large group of around thirty people there to welcome me "home." Aside from not having any visual knowledge of who these people were, I was sad about those I was not able to meet as they had passed away prior to my return – my Grandfather and Grandmother Perez, Uncle Frankie, Uncle Pepe and Auntie Da.

As I became acquainted with my family and met family friends, I would often hear about my mother. People would say:

"I knew your mother."

"She was so pretty and petite."

"She was always smiling and happy."

"She was so smart."

Everyone seemed to know something about her, except for me, her son. All I knew was that she had been killed at the end of the war on Guam. Thus, in an effort to get to know her, I began asking questions about her life. The more I learned, the more I wanted to know. As I gathered information, I thought her story might make a good book. I applied for and received a grant from the Insular Arts Council. Little did I know, writing this book would have a tremendous impact on my life.

Armed with the grant, I finally had the time to research and write the book. Aside from information I had received from my father, my mother's sister, Aunt Carmen was instrumental in helping me obtain much of the material I needed. She took me to meet and interview Mariquita's friends and those who worked with her at the Japanese agricultural camp in Tå'i.

When I first published *Mariquita – A Guam Story* thirty-seven years ago, I wrote in the preface that it was the most difficult project I had ever undertaken. Today, I still hold that same opinion. But if I had to do it again, I would most likely do it. Why? Because a greater force was pushing me to write it.

From the very beginning, *Mariquita* was difficult to write. One difficulty was finding all the written information I needed. Unlike today, it did not lie at one's fingertips and required a great deal of time and effort. I spent countless hours at the Nieves M. Flores Memorial Library in Hagåtña and at the Micronesian Area Research Center at the University of Guam gathering information and looking through old photos. My objective was to gather factual information and have an understanding of prewar Guam and Japan's occupation in order to imagine what it would have been like to live here during that time.

Another difficulty I had was that most of the people I interviewed, including family members, were reluctant to talk about the war as they were still trying to forget it. But they did open up. Not all the way, but as much as they could. In looking back now, I think they were more willing to be interviewed by me, because they knew I was a part of their wartime story.

The most difficult task, however, was to stay emotionally uninvolved. I thought I could simply write the book as an observer. In the beginning, I did just that, but as I got deeper into the written work, and with some documentary information I received, it became increasingly more difficult. Toward the end of the book, it became impossible, because I realized I was not just writing about a person, I was writing about my mother.

Also, toward the end of writing the book, my father and his wife BJ came to visit me. By the time he arrived on Guam, he was fully committed to what I was doing. In some way, I was helping him release all his pent-up feelings about the war. He wanted to see every chapter I had written and comment on everything, particularly the section about him. For example, prior to his visit, he wrote: "Something just struck me about your chapter. The <u>emotion</u> is missing! I can supply that. I remember, for example, how sad I was, probably big tears in my eyes, the last look I had of the ship. Down by the stern and the flag was just touching the water."

There were times when I found it difficult to balance his helping me with his bothering me. Focused on writing, I just hadn't seen how much he was giving of himself to help me and what it meant to him. During his visit, he got to see people he had known and visit places he had remembered. He thoroughly enjoyed his time here. Aside from our family barbeque, what I remember most is him putting his arm across my shoulders one evening while talking to me – something I can't recall him ever doing before.

My father also wrote to me about the genre I had chosen: "You have maintained that you are writing a novel," he wrote. "For that reason, I have had difficulty understanding why you want factual information. A novel is defined as 'a fictitious prose narrative … portraying characters.' Having read your Chapter, which I think is very, very good, I know you are not writing a novel. By the terms that I understand, you are writing a biography, defined as 'a written account of another person's life.' If you expand it enough, put in a lot of conversations that come only from your imagination, create situations that may or may not have ever existed, then you probably would have a fictionalized biography…" Although I agreed with his assessment, I didn't pay it much attention as all I wanted to do was finish the book and end the prolonged sadness I was experiencing.

The printing of the book was another big problem. There were no book printing or publishing places on Guam. Determined to have it done locally, I sought the help of my friend Lourdes "Lou" Perez. We formed PPH (Perez, Perez Howard) and Company. After talking to a number of printers of magazines and pamphlets, including one who printed the telephone book, I finally found someone up to the challenge. He said he would print 100 copies and all I had to do was supply him with photos and the finished manuscript.

I paid someone who was working at the University of Guam and who I thought was an expert to type the final manuscript. Trusting his work, I gave it to the printer. When the first printed copies came out, I was shocked to find so many typographical errors, I was almost ready to give up. But my "never say die" attitude prevailed. With the help of Lou and the printer, we worked diligently, sometimes at night, to make the necessary corrections and replace pages that needed to be replaced. So, if you are one of those who bought the first printing, I'm sorry you did not get a clean copy, and I'm sorry if some of the pages fell out due to the glue used to bind them. The book truly came to life during the very early days of printing and publishing on Guam.

After the first printing of *Mariquita*, I didn't have the resources or the local support I needed to republish the book. It was hard for me to believe that all the work I had done would end with those 100 books. The book, however, did not go unnoticed. Because of the book and my involvement in the nuclear free movement, I represented Guam at the First Hiroshima Conference of Asian Writers in Japan in 1983. The following year, *Mariquita* was translated and published in Japan. And in 1986, it was published by the University of the South Pacific under the title *Mariquita – A Tragedy of Guam*.

I also received a number of awards: The Chief Quipuha Award for "Outstanding Dedication and Contribution to Humanity by one of Chamorro ancestry" from the Honorable Governor Ricardo J. Bordallo; a Legislative Resolution for "involvement in preserving and promoting the Chamorro culture and traditions of Guam" and for the publication of *Mariquita - A Guam Story*; and an Onran I Espiriton Hurao Award from the University of Guam's Chamorro Association and Southern Comfort Club for Publication, Electronics, Media, and Organization.

Aside from some corrections and minor changes in subsequent publications under the publishing name Cyfred Ltd., I have not done a review of the book because of the emotional impact it had on me when I wrote it. But facing a relaunch of the book, and wanting it to be the best it can be, I felt it was time to thoroughly examine it, knowing that I was now better equipped to handle the emotional aspect of it.

Overall, in my review of the book, I was pleased with what I had written, but I also saw some things that needed to be addressed. This was made evident by my editor in some of her comments on the working draft of this edtion. The most important of these was that although I had captured the character of Mariquita, I had not done enough to reconcile the progressive island girl I had depicted with the outspoken, intellectual girl interviewed in *Collier's Magazine*.

This edition, *Mariquita - revisited*, aside from editorial changes and the blending of Mariquita's character, also corrects some misconceptions, provides more information, and reflects my better understanding of Chamorro culture and Guam history. As in previous publications, I have kept the term "Guamanian" and used the older spelling of Chamorro and Agana instead of CHamoru and Hagåtña to reflect the time period. I also included letters that were written by my father, mother and grandmother before, during and after the war. I inherited these cherished letters, which really capture the voices of my loved ones and the details of their lives.

This is the story of my mother.

1
Agana, 1938

HER BIRTH NAME WAS Maria Aguon Perez, but like other girls named Maria on the island of Guam, she was called Mariquita – "little Mary" – or Tita for short. Mariquita disliked the name Maria. As a little girl, she refused to sign her grade school papers with her given name, much to the vexation of her teacher who was also named Maria. Her teacher not only liked the name but thought it the only proper one to use on class papers. Yet no amount of cajoling or returned papers with "Mariquita" scratched out and "Maria" written instead could get the little girl to submit.

At eighteen years old, her name was no longer a problem. The year prior, Mariquita graduated from the first ninth grade class of George Washington Junior-Senior High School, which had opened in Agana in 1936. And then, being ambitious and eager to learn more, she enrolled in evening classes at the Guam Institute, a private school that offered vocational and academic classes, run by Nieves Flores. She took secretarial

Mariquita (second row, far left) on her graduation day in 1937. (M.A.R.C. Photo Collection)

courses and began working as a stenographer for B.J. Bordallo, a member of the Guam Congress, which served as an advisory council to the U.S. Naval governor. As his stenographer, she enjoyed the political discourse concerning the Navy's administration of the island and often engaged in conversation with Congress members. Mr. Bordallo also rented and sold cars, and operated one of the few taxi services on the island.

Being a stenographer was an unusual occupation for a young woman in 1938, as the only generally accepted female professions, aside from homemaking, were teaching and nursing. Mariquita had rejected these professions, preferring the business and political world. To this end, she was still taking evening classes at the Guam Institute.

On a slightly rainy Friday, she was able to leave work early. She did not have classes that evening and she was free to do whatever she wanted. She also had the weekend off, and was looking forward to the activities she had planned with her girlfriends. But at the moment, she just wanted to be by herself and had walked up Tutuhan Hill, overlooking Agana and the sea, to think and contemplate her future.

Mariquita was a lovely girl – both shapely and petite, she was a pleasing mixture of her diverse lineage and her native heritage. She was a direct descendent of a man, who was recorded to be the last known full-blooded Chamorro, and she was also part Spanish and Chinese. Her skin was warm brown, smooth and unblemished. Her shoulder-length, shiny black hair was curled in the latest fashion, pulled back to the sides away from her temples, and held in place by tiny white barrettes, framing a face that held all the beauty and mystery of the Pacific. But it was her eyes, which were most fascinating. Her eyes revealed that she was not the stereotypical island girl depicted in romantic literature. She was not uncomplicated or submissive.

A glint of fire danced in Mariquita's dark eyes and revealed her inner self. This fire reflected her spirit and her energy, and along with her actions, prompted one of her classmates to liken her to the

Chichirika – a small, quick, reddish brown-bird with a fantail edged in white that was continually fluttering and flirting.

Mariquita's fire also fueled her curiosity and determination, and if her actions had not been tempered by her keen intelligence and humor, she could have been irritatingly aggressive. But her combination of character traits made her one of the most popular girls in the capital village. She was smart, fun, modern and independent.

Taking another look at the horizon, Mariquita turned to leave thinking that one day she would travel across the ocean and see America. As she walked the distance through the grassy field toward the jungle path that separated her from the road and civilization, she glanced back at where she had stood on the hill and regretted having to leave. She came up here often, seeking solitude, and the inner rewards she received in her communion with nature stoked the fire burning within her.

Mariquita followed the steep coral road that curved gently into town. The afternoon sun was hot and beads of perspiration began to form on her forehead. Two Navy trucks passed on their way up the hill, the drivers waving and whistling. She smiled, almost laughing at their enthusiastic display, one that always amused her. The fine dust stirred up by the passing trucks settled lightly on her rust-and-white-print dress, and on her shoes that had been covered with the same fabric to match it.

At the bottom of the hill she paused briefly before entering the capitol city of Agana. Containing close to half of the island's 22,000 people, it had existed since the ancient Chamorros considered their islands to be the whole earth. From its humble beginnings of a few huts along the banks of a gentle river that flowed parallel to the shore before snaking into the awesome Pacific, it had been the heartbeat of the people.

Typhoons, earthquakes, and destructive high tides over the years had not destroyed the city, nor had the onslaught of the Spaniards who in the name of religion had all but wiped out her peaceful civilized society. Agana was like the sword grass growing on the high hills of Guam, strong, bendable and enduring.

Agana of 1938, while influenced by many nationalities, was mainly a composite of Chamorro, Spanish and American cultures. The Chamorro people had changed with each new occupying power and many of the city's characteristics reflected this change, but the nature of the city remained faithful to the Chamorro heritage.

In other places in the world, a highly visible mixture of dissimilar material cultures in one city often creates an unpleasant picture, but such was not the case in Agana. It was as if some mystical hand had placed everything as precisely as a decorator would have in a room of mixed furnishings, and as colorfully as a florist when creating a mixed bouquet.

Agana lay on the western shore in central Guam. From atop the steep ridge of hills forming its backdrop, the city appeared below as a stage facing its audience, the ocean. The city streets were of gravel made from coral limestone, called *kaskåhu*, and were neatly maintained by the island's few prisoners. Some streets, including Hernan Cortez Street, commonly called Main Street, had been macadamized to keep the dust down when an occasional automobile or carabao cart passed.

The streets, not uniformly laid out as in American cities to form symmetrical blocks, posed a geometric puzzle to the Naval administrators who had governed Guam since the end of the 19th century.

In 1898, Guam became a possession of the United States upon the signing of the Treaty of Peace between the United States and Spain. The entire island was designated a naval station under the administrative authority of the Department of the Navy, which was also responsible for its government. Steps were immediately taken to create military order out of what must have appeared to be exotic chaos, and military scrutiny was extended to all aspects of island life. It was a confusing period for both the military and the islanders, and certainly a comedy for the observer.

In the ensuing *opera bouffe*, the islanders, having been under Spanish dominance for over 300 years, had to face a new language, a new currency, and a new kind of bureaucracy. The military, on the other hand, was faced with a tropical climate, a shy and fun-loving people, who had their own distinct traditions and culture. Complicating the situation further were the military's disdain for compromise and the islanders' unwillingness to accept forced change. After forty years, this improbable relationship appeared to work, mainly because the islanders had no choice and the military demanded it.

By the time Mariquita had reached the city limits at the foot of the hill, she decided to go to Elliott's Drug Store for a cool drink. She crossed the Plaza de España, heading for Main Street. The Plaza was beautiful, occupying two city blocks and fringed with towering palm trees and lush hibiscus hedges. The grass, kept short and green with continual care, was laced with concrete walks. In its center was a small, white bandstand with a Spanish-tiled roof, its weathered terra cotta

Layout of 1930s Agana with Plaza de España at the center (top). (M.A.R.C. Photo Collection) School children in the Plaza (middle). (M.A.R.C. Manuscripts) Native school children preforming a play for Naval Administrators and their wives (bottom). (M.A.R.C. Manuscripts)

color a soft complement to the splendor of the majestic flame trees. Surrounding the Plaza were the Dulce Nombre de Maria Cathedral; the St. Vincent de Paul building; the Government House, which was called the Governor's Palace because it contained his office; the Dorn Hall School; the Leary School; the police station; the Bank of Guam; the library and other government buildings.

The elementary school children were just being dismissed, and Mariquita could not help but notice the pageantry before her. The children began their frolicsome crossing of the Plaza lawns, their madrigal sounds filling the air. The little girls were in white dresses, the boys in white shirts and blue denim pants. Mariquita looked for her brother Felix among the children, but did not see him until she left the Plaza and crossed the street to the Leary School where he was a student. She found him under the old mammea tree in the school-yard, playing with his classmates. When he saw her, he grinned and ran excitedly to her.

"Tita, can I go swimming at the bridge today? Please?"

"You'll have to ask Mama," she replied taking his hand.

"But she doesn't get home until later. All my friends are going now. Please, Mariquita?" Felix pleaded.

"Don't you want to go with me for ice cream instead?" she asked.

"Oh, Tita, can't I go swimming?" he begged, ignoring her tempting offer. "Just today, please?"

Agana River. (M.A.R.C. Photo Collection)

"Okay, Felix," she relented, "but first you have to go home and get your bathing suit. Mama doesn't like you swimming at the bridge without one."

The bridge they were referring to was a Spanish bridge, a picturesque relic from the past that crossed the canal-like Agana River near the center of the city. The boys often went swimming there, diving from the bridge into the fresh water mixed with the clear, warm water released from the cooling system of the power plant next to it. This impossible structure, fueled by coal brought to the island and piled high in the Agana Navy Yard nearby, had a smoke stack 9 feet in diameter and 150 feet high. It was visible from any point in the city and the surrounding area.

"And don't forget to put your school clothes up," she cautioned. He started to leave, but she held his hand firmly. "Wait a minute," she added. "Don't stay out late or we'll both get in trouble. Be home before it gets dark or I'll send Johnny after you. You understand?" He nodded and ran happily to his friends as soon as she released his hand.

After the boys took off in all directions, some toward the bridge, Felix toward home, Mariquita became pensive as she thought about her responsibilities as the elder child in the family. Besides having to set an example, she often had to make decisions concerning her sister and five brothers, since both of her parents worked. She was glad Uncle Felipe, "Pepe," and Aunt Natividad, "Da," had come to live with them, as they relieved many of the household problems and restrictions which otherwise would have been on her.

Upon reaching the Elks Club, she turned onto San Ignacio Street, which ran parallel to Main Street. She wanted to enjoy her quiet walk just a little longer before coming to the business section where she would undoubtedly meet people she intimately knew and would have to stop and talk to them. San Ignacio Street was like many residential streets in the city. The narrow street was lined with a visual history of Guam's architecture. It ranged from the many simple wooden houses set on pilings, with steep front steps, shuttered windows, and pitched roofs of woven coconut fronds, to the modern two-story reinforced concrete house. In between were attractive Spanish-style houses with white-stuccoed walls, balconies and red-tiled roofs. A number of these also had two stories, and like their counterparts on Main Street, had a business on the ground floor.

In addition, there were a number of innovations and mixtures of styles. One, called *tabique*, had walls of evenly spaced dark-stained wood uprights, with the spaces between them filled with cement and painted white. The pitched roof was made of woven palm fronds, tiles, or tin. Though poorly constructed, this particular style was attractive. Picket fences or colorful croton hedges surrounded many of the houses, and the juxtaposition of the different styles along the street made Agana interesting and charming. The people's pride was apparent in the neatness and upkeep of their houses and was encouraged by the monthly military inspection of the city.

Nearing the drug store, Mariquita turned at the corner toward Main Street. A skinny brown dog was lying in the middle of the road, oblivious to a cautious mother hen and her chicks edging past it. The dog did not move even when Mariquita passed, but it did open a wary eye when some young men approached in the opposite direction. Mariquita greeted them, and then stopped for a while to talk with a couple of older women sitting on the steps of a house.

Agana had a small-town atmosphere. The people Mariquita met, other than visitors and newcomers to the island, were either relatives or acquaintances. This provided her with a sense of belonging, but it was also a deterrent to any private life she may have wanted.

Main Street, the principal business street in the city, although still retaining its native character, was gradually becoming like main streets in small towns across the United States. The change reflected the Americanization of Guam that much of the populace eventually embraced.

As Mariquita was entering Elliott's Drug Store in the Martinez Building, a young sailor whom she had met some

Pre-war Agana architecture. (M.A.R.C. Photo Collection)

time ago and was now trying to avoid, surprised her. For the past several weeks, he had been openly following her around town. When they first met, she had enjoyed the attention he gave her and had encouraged it by flirting back, a favorite pastime of Mariquita and her girlfriends – second only to the movies. Now, realizing the extent of his interest, she was cautious of his attention and had begun to shy away from him. But instead of the response she expected – a loss of interest – she saw his infatuation was growing and his presence began to bother her. What bothered her most was the awareness that she was the cause of his gloom, as well as his happiness, and lately he showed more of the former.

"Hafa Adai, Mariquita," the young sailor said, using the Chamorro greeting he had obviously carefully rehearsed.

"Hafa Adai, Eddie. I see you are learning Chamorro. The last time we met you only knew hafa," she said jokingly. "You are off duty today?"

"Mariquita, would you like to go to the movies with me this evening?" he blurted.

Surprised by this unexpected invitation, it took Mariquita a few moments to answer. "I'm sorry Eddie, but my mother will not let me date. Besides, I already promised my girlfriends. Thank you anyway."

"Well, ah, I'll probably see you later at the movies. See you," he said nervously as he turned and left the store. "Bye, Eddie," Mariquita called after him, feeling guilty like she always did after seeing him. He left her with a sense that she was either hurting him or would eventually. Deep down, Mariquita thought hurting him would be inevitable. It wasn't that she didn't like Eddie; she just wasn't inter-ested in developing a relationship with an American, something she knew her father would be against. Besides, she already had a few local admirers she had to deal with. She took a deep breath and then spied Marian, one of her closest friends since graduating from eighth grade, beckoning to her from one of the booths at the soda fountain section of the store. She quickly went and sat down across from her.

Marian Johnston was Mariquita's confidant. She was the daughter of an American serviceman and a Chamorro educator. Since her father's discharge from the service, he had settled amicably into civilian life, and had become a successful businessman. Among the several businesses he owned was the popular movie house, the Gaiety Theater on Main Street. Her mother, Agueda, was a highly respected educator and the principal of George Washington High School. Opened in 1936, it was the only public high school on the island.

Being the daughter of such prominent citizens created a few problems for Marian, but it also opened a few doors. She was the most socially minded of her friends, in part because of her parents' acceptance into the military's inner social circle. Although a few accused her of having "airs" because she usually spoke English, she was popular and often took her girlfriends with her to the "by invitation only" military functions. Sometimes at these functions, and at various other social affairs in the city, she would be part of the entertainment, performing Hawaiian dances she had learned at dancing school.

Marian was an attractive girl with dark-brown curly hair and a fair complexion. Although by American standards of height, she would have been considered average, by local standards she was tall, and when standing next to the petite, cute Mariquita, she sometimes felt a little awkward. She had excellent manners, was a good conversationalist, and like Mariquita, was outspoken and had a strong, determined personality. This at times put Marian and Mariquita at odds, but it did not interfere with their friendship since they mutually understood and respected one another. Together, they initiated many of their group's activities and stabilized the group's relationships.

"Marian, what am I going to do about Eddie? He just keeps after me."

"He's really a nice guy, Mariquita. I don't know why you don't like him," Marian replied, sensing her friend's frustration.

"I know he's nice. That's what makes it worse. I have to be nice back to him. He must know I'm not crazy about him. I treat him like the others. I mean, I do like him, but that's all."

"Mariquita, don't let it bother you. Maybe he just wants to be friends," Marian said encouragingly.

"Friends! You mean you haven't seen that gleam in his eyes?" Mariquita asked, then continued melodramatically. "It says 'undying love' and 'I want to take you away from it all.' Marian, there is nothing I want to leave!"

"Oh, Mariquita, you should be an actress. Now settle down. Would you like a soda?"

"Oh, yes, I guess so. That's why I came here in the first place. I'll have a Coke, thank you. It's so hot." Mariquita leaned back in the booth grateful for the breeze from the ceiling fan overhead. Marian went to the counter, got the Coke and returned.

"By the way, Mariquita, where have you been? At the office they told me you had gotten off early, and I have been searching for you all around town," Marian asked as she sat.

"Just around – actually, I went for a walk. Can't you tell by my dusty self?" Mariquita said. She took a sip of her drink, looking pensive and secretive.

"Well, you didn't go to the dressmaker's, Margaret said you hadn't been at the beauty shop, and you were not shopping at Butler's Department Store," Marian continued prying. "Where have you been?"

Teasingly, Mariquita asked, "Is that all you think I come to town for?"

"Mariquita, are you seeing somebody?" Marian asked outright.

"Of course not. I couldn't hide anything from you if I wanted to. Now, what are we going to do about Eddie?"

"We? You are not getting me in the middle of this one. Remember Franklin, the one you said you liked – the one who looked like Errol Flynn? As your friend I had to entertain him when you were no longer interested in talking to him. Mariquita, that was the last one! You're always changing your mind."

"I can't help it. I like to flirt. Anyway, most of them, once you get to know them, have nothing to say, and those that are a little interesting seem to just want to get you in a dark corner and all that lovey-dovey business."

"Mariquita, you just haven't met the right one yet."

"Honestly, Marian, do you think there is a right one? Now, what can I do about Eddie? He is sweet, and I don't want to hurt his feelings. Are you sure you're not interested? Just a little bit?"

"I'm not interested, and I know he is not interested in me. He was sitting here a while before you came and all he talked about was you: what you liked to do, how cute you were, if you were serious about anyone. Of course, I told him nothing."

"I bet," Mariquita said, not believing her for a minute. Playing with the straw in her drink, she said abruptly, "That's it! All I have to do is show that I'm interested in someone else. And then you can just tell him." Sighing, she added, "But who?"

"Mariquita, there is a new ship coming in December. There will be plenty to choose from."

"December! December is five months away, Marian. No, something has to be done soon. I could become unavailable – but that wouldn't be any fun. Well, I'll come up with something. Do you think Delia might like him?"

"Delia likes that blond sailor from California, the one with the muscles. Did you see how tight his shirt was the other day and how he kept showing off? I don't know what she sees in him, but then again, I guess I do. Did you know I had to see the last Tarzan movie at the Agana Theater with her twice because she wanted to be with him?"

"Is that right? And she told me she had only seen it once when she asked me to go with her to the last showing. That Delia!"

"Yes, we've got to do something about Delia. Last month it was cowboys she liked. It's hard to dress up and be sophisticated with Delia's boyfriends around. Remember the one who wanted her to see how a real live cowboy looked? That outfit! And all those kids following us," Marian said. Both girls started laughing as they recalled that evening, with Delia enjoying the display and the rest of them trying to keep from laughing. "I wonder where he got those clothes," she added.

When their laughter subsided, Mariquita suddenly said, "Marian, I have to go! I almost forgot, we're going to have fish tonight and I told Auntie Da I would be home to help her. If you're ready I'll walk you home."

"Mariquita, that reminds me. Do you still eat salted salmon with cake?"

"Marian, as always, you have no idea what is good for you. It's something you don't understand. Any intelligent person eats salted salmon with cake."

"Ugh, you go ahead. I have some shopping to do for mother. Come to my house at six. I already told the other two."

"Okay, bye now." Mariquita started to leave, then stopped and asked, "Are we going to wear what we planned?"

"Yes, and don't forget the hat. It will be so exciting, and I can hardly wait to show our new outfits. I'll see you later."

The other two girls they were meeting that evening were Delia Ada and Carolyn Mayhew. Delia was a cousin to Mariquita and resembled her in appearance. Her parents owned a soap factory, and both of them were Chamorro. Delia had large brown eyes and a big smile. Nothing seemed to bother her. She was very friendly with an uncomplicated personality and she took everything in stride. Because of this, and her ability to laugh easily at herself, she was sometimes the loving target of the other girls' kidding. She was the youngest of the group after a fifth member, Lourdes Murphy, had left for the United States. She was always busy, the only one of the girls who had regular chores to do at home. Delia enjoyed life, and especially liked her job as an usher at the Gaiety Theater.

Like Marian, Carolyn was the daughter of an American businessman and a Guamanian woman. Among the businesses they owned was the Mayhew Ice Cream Parlor on Main Street, and like the parents of the other girls, they were relatively well off.

Carolyn was a pretty girl with light brown hair and looked every bit American. She had more freedom than her girlfriends to the extent that she was allowed to date unchaperoned and have her boyfriend visit her at her house. This gave her a certain edge over the others in terms of being modern, but it also gave rise to gossip. She had an adventurous, outgoing personality, and her behavior was at times unconventional. No one forgot the time she and Lourdes Murphy took a boat and paddled down the Agana River to the ocean, proceeding along the coast where they eventually had to be picked up because they were too tired to paddle back. She was always fun to be around.

Agana at that time was a peaceful and wonderful place to live. It had achieved that perfect balance of having neither too much nor too little. In such an environment, it was no wonder that the four girls had such a zest for life. They had every opportunity for happiness, and they were taking advantage of these opportunities. All that was required was their own self-motivation, and they had plenty of that. They had known each other since childhood and formed bonds of intimate friendship stronger than any they might have in the future. They cared about one another, and it was with each other that they faced life and dreamed their dreams. How could they possibly know that fate would so cruelly separate them?

2

A Composite Culture

MARIQUITA'S FAMILY LIVED at 715 Dr. Sargent Street in the Dr. Sargent District located in the northwestern section of the city along the ocean. Formerly called Bilibic, a name of unknown origin, it was changed by popular consent because of its similarity to Bilibid, the infamous prison in Manila. The name chosen was in honor of Lieutenant William Snow Sargent, a surgeon in the U.S. Medical Corps who served on Guam from 1929 to 1931.

The Perez home was a modem two-story concrete house. The ground floor consisted of a large kitchen-and-dining-room combination, a living room, two smaller rooms, a bathroom, and an open terrace. The upper floor contained the family's living quarters. Situated on an attractively landscaped lot, it faced the quaint street with structural dignity. Behind the house, the view was a special composition of earth, sea and sky.

Mariquita's parents were teachers at the Government Industrial School. Their combined income had enabled them to move from a modest house behind the Leary School to their new home, which had all the modern conveniences. Still, when the power failed, the Perez family had to rely upon old methods – they caught rainwater from the roof in 50-gallon drums and had kerosene lamps ready. They appreciated their new home, as many families still used the communal bathhouse, water station, and outhouses.

Josefa Unpingco Aguon, Mariquita's mother, had managed her

home well since marrying Juan Taijeron Perez and bearing him seven children. She was a tall, proud woman who had come from a prosperous native family that included a Chinese ancestor, Un Pian Co, whose name evolved into the last name Unpingco. Her nickname, which most people knew more than her given name, was derived from her mother's father, Rosauro Unpingco. Josefa was called "Pai Sauro" – Pai, the nickname for Josefa, and Sauro a shortening of her grandfather's name. The rest of the family also had nicknames and pet names, often of a humorous nature.

Mama Pai had long, straight black hair which she knotted at the nape of her neck, and like most women her age, wore the popular cotton day dresses except on Sundays and holidays when the *mestiza* was worn. The mestiza consisted of a low-necked blouse with large bell sleeves made of *piña* cloth or fine net worn over a lace or embroidered camisole, and a long, colorful, cotton skirt. A headscarf and beaded slippers usually completed the outfit. Mama Pai had a progressive yet protective outlook concerning her family and ran the house with authority.

Thanks to Mama Pai's facility for learning, and her parents' foresight in seeing the advantages of having their children learn English after the Americans took over the island, she was ready when the military government began recruiting islanders to take over the teaching duties of U.S. government personnel and expanded vocational classes.

Teaching suited Mama Pai's personality and creative mind. She taught sewing and weaving, and particularly enjoyed teaching *akgak* weaving classes. She and her pupils used the dried leaves of the pandanus plant to make purses, mats, fans, and numerous baskets and other articles that they later sold, giving the proceeds back to the school. Mama Pai was also a prominent member of the Guam Teachers Association. Among the Association's activities were benefit balls, boxing, and other entertainment for charity; volunteer work for the American Red Cross and the Susana Hospital; fundraising for community projects; and the sponsoring of musical operettas such as the *Princess of Chrysanthemum*, *El Toroso*, and *Bel of Santa Magarita*.

The classes that Mama Pai and her husband Juan taught at the Industrial School were required subjects for all city school students in grades five through nine. The boys were taught carpentry and net making, the girls cooking and sewing. Both girls and boys had to take weaving and gardening. Juan was one of the carpentry teachers, and later was sent by the government to the Philippines to learn the art of making rattan furniture. This craft would become a part of the curriculum.

Juan, or "Papa," was a mild mannered, stable man who considered himself fortunate in having met and married Mama Pai. He was one of his mother Carmen's five children. His father, a native-born whaler of mixed ancestry, was not a member of Papa's immediate household in Chalan Pago, but he knew him and was given his name.

The responsibility of the household rested on the shoulders of Papa's grandfather, Regino Tajito Taijeron. From him, Papa learned gardening and carpentry, which he liked because he enjoyed working with his hands. When his grandfather and mother died, he inherited part of the family property in the small farming community three miles from Agana.

On the property, with the help of family and friends, he built a typical native ranch house with a corrugated tin roof that was practical, and to him, made music when it rained. He spent his weekends there, happy to be away from the city, sometimes with one of his sons and Mama Pai's cousin Pepe. He grew vegetables, gathered wild fruits from the jungle and had some chickens, a few pigs, and a carabao. His brother Vicente or "Ben" as he was called, lived on the adjoining property and took care of the animals when he was away. The ranch was also the scene of family gatherings. They would go there by carabao cart, or if they planned well in advance, in Uncle Juan Aguon's jitney.

Life was good for the Perez family, and there were few worries. Aside from Joseph, who had just turned five, and Mariquita, who was out of school and working, the rest of the children were in school and doing well. Sixteen-year-old Johnny was the eldest son. He was a strong young man, capable of handling almost any situation. Frankie, younger by two years, was sports-minded, playing on the popular Riverside basketball and baseball teams. Walter, next in age, had a stable, popular personality. He loved fishing and was known for his skill in spear fishing. At nine, the fourth son Felix already showed an aptitude for learning and was thought to be the studious one of the children. Six-year old Carmen, the only other girl, was pretty and delightful, and was becoming increasingly spoiled by all the attention she received from her brothers and sister. Joseph, the youngest, was quiet and mischievous, but he rarely got into trouble.

It took strong and loving hands to run a large native family. Mama Pai and Papa ran theirs by demanding strict obedience and giving tender caresses. Although Mama Pai was in authority, Papa always had the final say. Foremost in their teachings was religious training, which included daily prayers and religious ceremonies in the home.

Native life revolved around the Catholic Church. Besides the mass and religious ceremonies in the church and home, the Perez family took an active part in the religious life of the community. They always participated in solemn processions and pageants. Feasts were often a part of these observances with extended family gatherings to celebrate weddings and baptisms, and to pay last respects when someone died.

Actually, any cause for a celebration called for a fiesta. Much of the food preparation and other work was done by those close to the family. An elaborate table would be set with an array of tempting dishes: succulent roast pig, chicken, seafood, red rice, and depending on the season, various kinds of local root crops, leafy vegetables and fruits. Many of these dishes were of Spanish, Mexican or Philippine origin, often hot and spicy. Great pride was taken in the abundance and quality of the food. These fiestas were commonly held outdoors under the protective covering of thatched palm fronds, and sometimes were accompanied by music and dancing. The people attending were friends, relatives and neighbors, and on special occasions, such as a feast day to honor a village's patron saint, everyone would be welcome.

Aside from the church, education was the most important part of the Perez family's life. Mama Pai and Papa realized that their economic and social status depended upon it. In the last years of Mariquita's schooling, she was not required to do any household chores as long as she was studying. Her only responsibilities were too see that the chores were done and to help discipline and supervise the younger children. This did not require much effort since they had all been rigidly taught to respect their elders; however, if there were any problems, she would grab the *eskoban nuhot*, a broom made out of the spines of a coconut frond, and swat the offender. Mariquita had a prominent position in the home, and she was not shy to demonstrate it.

Despite the special emphasis placed on learning the English language, Chamorro was spoken in the home. This balanced, to some extent, the requirement that only English was to be spoken in school and on the playground, as well as in government and public affairs. By 1939, most of the Guamanian population was bilingual, speaking English and Chamorro. Auntie Da, who rarely left the house, and those of the older generation spoke only their native tongue, some also speaking their former possessor's Spanish.

When Mariquita arrived home, Da was already preparing the fish. She was in a separate structure built on the ocean side of the house to catch the passing breeze. It contained cooking and laundry facilities, and had a large Spanish beehive oven, or hotno, nearby where many delectable dishes were cooked. It was a favorite place for the children to eat and to entertain friends, and it was here that Da prepared most of the family meals, preferring to cook over the familiar wood fire rather than use the new kerosene stove in the house.

Auntie Da, Natividad Aguon Unpingco, was blind. She was Mama Pai's double first cousin; an Unpingco brother and sister married an Aguon brother and sister. She and Mama Pai had a close relationship much like sisters, Mama Pai being the elder. Before Da became blind in her late teens, she moved in with Mama Pai's family, taking her younger brother Pepe with her, an action not unusual since people frequently went to live with a relative's family, the extended family being closely bound by social, economic and religious ties and customs.

Da became an integral part of the Perez family, and although she became totally blind, capably handled many of the household duties including cooking, washing and ironing. She helped the whole family and enabled Mama Pai to continue her teaching career, thus adding to the family's finances. Da also became a surrogate mother to all the children, particularly Walter, who was born shortly after her arrival and whom she considered almost to be her own.

When Mariquita returned home she greeted Da with a kiss on the back of the neck, causing her to giggle and jokingly exclaim, "Mariquita, you better watch out, I have a knife in my hand!" Laughing, Mariquita teased Da, "You probably heard me coming from the time I left the store." Seeing that Da did not need any help, Mariquita sat down on one of the benches and watched the older woman expertly clean the remainder of the fish that Walter had caught that morning. Da looked pretty as she stood against the late afternoon sky, her hair in a loose knot, and dressed in a simple white-cotton blouse and a long, faded, calico skirt. Mariquita had been fascinated by Da ever since she had moved in with the family when Mariquita was seven years old. She was especially intrigued by how Da could remain so cheerful in her condition with so little prospect of any change in her life.

At home, meals were informal, but they were one of the ways Mama Pai and Papa kept track of their large family as permission had to be granted for anyone to be absent. During the week the family usually ate together, but on weekends they ate separately or in twos and threes, depending on what activities were going on. Food was always available at any time of the day for anyone, including visitors. Since food did not keep long in the icebox without spoiling, the children often had to run errands to get things. If there was a large quantity of food or some special delicacy, like *fanihi* or *ayuyu*, some would be given to friends and relatives.

What was thrown out went to the few chickens and dogs the family kept.

By five o'clock that day, everyone had returned home and the table was set. Besides the customary pot of rice and *fina'denne'*, there was fish in a broth of lemon juice and coconut milk spiced with onions, garlic and fresh pepper, some taro and eggplant, and papaya from the ranch.

After eating hurriedly, Mariquita went upstairs to the room she shared with Carmen. It was a pleasant room with an *ifit* wood floor kept pristinely polished by the children, who scrubbed it with coconut husks as one of their regular chores. The room was large and had shuttered windows on the outside walls. The windows were usually left open for cross ventilation, and the breeze would sway the delicate lace curtains, one of Mariquita's prized possessions, given to her by her nina.

Papa had made most of the furniture in the room, including the twin beds that Mariquita had covered in blue gingham. On her bureau were her cosmetics, some perfume, toilet articles, a radio and an old doll that Mama Pai had made for her from a sock when Mariquita was a baby. Above her bureau was a mirror from which hung her rosary beads and taped around the frame, some photographs.

Throughout the room were various mementos: a ribbon from her first communion, a medal for "Best Weaving" from the American Legion and a pressed plumeria flower. It was a very feminine room, full of softness and remembrances. It was also a room that showed Mariquita's interest in reading, as there were a number of books and magazines, and her passion for fashion. Clothes filled the bureau drawers and the two large closets. Heaped on a sewing table next to one of the windows were dress patterns, more articles of clothing and scraps of material. Mariquita also had a large assortment of accessories: shoes, handbags, hats and scarves in a variety of styles and colors.

At a time when many of the girls in the rural areas had only two dresses, one for everyday wear and one for church, Mariquita had an excessive amount. This was not only because of her financial position, but also because of her ability to sew. She loved new things and kept up with the latest trends that she saw pictured in magazines and in the movies. She gave away many of the clothes that she no longer wore, always replacing them with something new. Besides sewing for herself, she knew several seamstresses in Agana who needed only a picture to inexpensively produce exquisite garments.

Not wanting to be seen wearing the same thing often required a large wardrobe, and since there were several social functions and movies each week, she needed several changes.

Her interest in fashion was one she shared with her girlfriends, and there was competition among the girls as to who had the newest outfit and the latest style. It was a friendly competition, but at times it produced some rather strange outfits, like the ones they had planned to wear that night.

One of Mariquita's many stylish outfits.
(Perez Howard Photo Collection)

Apart from their interest in fashion, Mariquita and her girlfriends were involved in community projects. They were always among the first ones asked to assist, whether it was for a benefit for the American Red Cross or to raise funds for uniforms for one of the local close-order-drill teams. Whatever they were involved in, they enjoyed. Life for them was fun and full of variety.

Mariquita was excited to meet the girls that night. They had planned to go to the Plaza for the evening band concert and then to the movie theater. Although Marian and Delia had to work after the concert – Marian selling tickets for her family's theater and Delia as an usher – they were allowed to leave their posts and join their friends as soon as the audience was seated and the movie had begun. Because it offered a little privacy, the girls would go and sit in the balcony. Their admirers would be waiting for them, and after some shifting of seats to enable each girl to sit beside her current favorite, some handholding would take place. Those who were truly enamored might indulge in a little light necking. This was done with innocence and with the awareness that "people talk." Also, Mrs. Johnston kept an eye on the balcony.

When Mariquita was satisfied that her outfit was just right, she hurried downstairs to inform her parents that she was leaving. It had taken her hair so long to dry that she knew she was going to be late, but she was not worried because punctuality was rarely expected. The girls were always on Chamorro Time.

Most of the supper dishes had been cleared away, but Mariquita's parents were still at the dining table talking to Pepe. They stopped talking as soon as they saw her.

"What is that you are wearing?" Mama Pai asked in amazement.

"A suit, Mama," Mariquita responded. "It's one of the new styles. All of us girls are wearing the same sort of style tonight."

"It looks warm. And are you sure that's the way you are supposed to look?"

"It's exactly like in the magazine, Mama. It's for the evening, and it's really not that warm. I can take off the jacket if it gets hot. See?" Mariquita said, taking off the jacket and making a few turns.

"You look like one of the roosters with that feather in your hat, Tita," Pepe chimed in.

"That feather is from your rooster, Pepe. You should be honored that I'm wearing it."

"Not my best fighting rooster?" he cried out in mock pain.

"Yep, and it was the nicest one he had!"

Papa laughed but didn't say anything. He was used to seeing his daughter in strange outfits. He approved no matter what she wore, because he had complete confidence in her selections. To him, Mariquita was the perfect daughter and he was very proud of her.

"I guess it is all right," Mama Pai said. "Now don't be late. If your girlfriends can't walk you home, be sure you come home with Frankie. He's going to the movies, too. I'll wait up for you. And tell Mrs. Johnston that I'll get the school report for the newspaper over to her soon."

"Okay, Mama. Bye, everyone."

"Tita, the rooster looked better with the feather than you do!" Pepe called out as Mariquita was leaving. He liked to tease her as she was genuinely good-natured and always had an answer for everything.

"Pepe, your rooster never looked this good. In fact, it's going to look better in the cooking pot tomorrow!" she answered as she jauntily left the room.

Mariquita was greeted by the porcelain blue sky that had already become streaked with red and gold from the setting sun. There were many people outdoors, some sitting on house steps and others standing in groups talking. She greeted people amicably, and they in turn paid great attention to her attire.

The other girls were already there when she reached Marian's house on Main Street. There were a lot of exclamations over each other's outfits, since each girl had kept secret what she planned to wear. The only thing they had agreed on in advance was that they would all wear hats. There was no clear winner, each having worn an exact copy of a new fashion seen in some recent magazine. However, they agreed that Carolyn had a slight edge over them. In truth, they all appeared a bit strange for Guam.

Carolyn was a vision in polka dots, navy blue on a cream background. Her padded shoulders were enhanced by a large artificial mum of brilliant yellow at the right of her throat. Her three-quarter-length sleeves were banded at the bottom to give an overall puffed effect. Her

waist was cinched with a narrow, yellow belt to match her
flower. Topping off her outfit
was a pancake-shaped hat,
also yellow, which drooped
demurely over one eye.

Marian's hat was helmet-
shaped and matched the ivory
color of her dress. She was the
picture of sophistication in a
solid two-piece gabardine
dress with a large collar that

Mariquita, Delia, Marian and Carolyn ready for a night out. (Johnston Family Photo Collection)

parted at the neck to reveal a bouquet of violets. Her loose fitted skirt was banded at the waist, and like the other girls, it hung almost to her ankles.

Delia wore a dusty-rose colored suit. The jacket's front was all collar, angled and opened to the waist. On this enormous collar was pinned a frilly white handkerchief to match her white blouse. The jacket hung long in the back but was cut away in the front resembling a man's tailcoat. On her head was a pert beret, and she wore the open-toed pumps of the time.

Mariquita's suit was simpler than Delia's. Over a white blouse she wore a bell-sleeved pale-gray jacket with a large V-shaped collar that extended over and past her shoulders making them appear exception-ally broad. The jacket was fitted at the waist, and then hung loosely over a long skirt. Her cone-shaped hat was the same color as her suit, with the exquisite blue-green feather matching the jacket's lining.

After completing their complimentary exchanges, the four friends walked to the Plaza, chattering and joking. The band was playing when they arrived and a large number of people were walking through the Plaza grounds and sitting on plaza benches. The band, composed of local musicians led by an American bandmaster, was playing the popular music that was regularly featured at the Friday evening concerts. The program would likely include music by Benny Goodman and Tommy Dorsey. On other evenings, the band would play marches, waltzes, classical music and occasionally something local such as Dr. Ramon Sablan's *Recuerdos de Ayer.* On weekday mornings the band played spirited tunes and marches while the school children did their morning exercises in the Plaza.

The girls, their outfits commanding a lot of attention, promenaded around the Plaza several times, smiling and acknowledging comments and ignoring the giggling and laughter from some of the young boys. They stopped at a bench occupied by some of their former classmates and chatted with them for a while before occupying a bench nearby. The pause gave them a chance to talk to each other about whom they had seen and what maneuvers they should make in order to make contact with the ones they wanted to meet.

"Did you see Robert and Philip over there on the bench in front of the Governor's Palace?" Carolyn asked Marian, excitedly.

"Yes, I did. And Mariquita, Eddie is there, too," Marian added.

"Let's walk over that way again," prompted Carolyn.

"You two go ahead. Delia and I will stay here. All right, Delia?" Mariquita asked, taking Delia's hand. "I don't want to encourage Eddie." Although Delia would have preferred going, she stayed behind with Mariquita.

Marian and Carolyn strolled casually ahead in the direction of the young sailors who appeared to be listening to the music but were keeping a sharp eye out for the girls. The girls intentionally appeared to be walking past them, when one of the sailors called to Marian and got up to greet her. Marian's heart beat faster.

"Hi Marian. Why don't you girls come here and sit with us? It's a nice night, isn't it?"

"Robert, how are you?" Marian said, acting surprised, as if she hadn't noticed him before. "We really can't now, but you could join us later," she said, waving a hello to the other sailors and smiling at the young man who was approaching Carolyn. "We're just seeing who's around and enjoying the music before the movie starts."

"Marian, you look great ... and so do you Carolyn. Don't forget that I'll be saving you a seat at the movies."

The other sailors were getting up to join them, but the two girls felt compelled to leave because of appearances. It was better if the men came to them; otherwise, they would appear to be picking them up. They smiled and continued on, returning to their friends. Marian, barely able to control her excitement, burst out, "Mariquita, Robert is such a dream! I could hardly talk to him. Is my hat all right?"

"Yes, you look fine. Oh, no don't look now but here comes Auntie Luisa. She hasn't stopped watching us since we arrived. She doesn't approve of us talking to the Americans." As the old woman in her mestiza came up to them, Marian backed away.

"Hafa Adai, Auntie Luisa?" Mariquita said as she got up from the bench and respectfully sniffed the old woman's hand. "You look very nice tonight. Are you enjoying the music?"

"Things aren't like they used to be," she complained as the band struck up "Harbor Lights."

"Too many foreigners here. The old ways are changing, and it's not good."

"Auntie Luisa, you are worrying too much. Many nice things are happening to our island. How's Uncle Jose?"

"He's still sick. The *taotaomo'na* is not happy. I told him to be more respectful and not drink so much tuba, but he don't listen."

Over Auntie Luisa's shoulder, Mariquita could see the young sailors approaching. She wished she could hide, as she knew that Auntie Luisa would be sure to tell her mother and exaggerate the entire incident. Although Mariquita knew that her mother would not believe everything the old woman said, she still did not like Auntie Luisa putting unnecessary thoughts in her mother's head. Mariquita respected Auntie Luisa, as she had been taught, but Auntie Luisa was bitter and meddlesome, and at times Mariquita had to use all her self-control to keep from telling her off.

Trying to lure the old woman away, Mariquita took a few steps away from her friends in the direction of the old woman's companions, but Auntie Luisa would not move. It was only after the sailors arrived and surrounded Mariquita's friends that she left, giving Mariquita a look of marked disapproval that would have ruined the evening of a girl less emotionally strong.

Knowing Eddie was there did not help the situation, but automatically Mariquita's face brightened as she reacted to the enjoyment of her friends.

Proper decorum prohibited girls and boys from sitting together, so the two groups remained divided as they listened to the concert. By now the Plaza was patterned by the warm glow of electric lights and softened by the tropical moon overhead. The concert continued with the band playing, "Let's Sail to Dreamland" and "Love Walked In."

After the concert, a parade of young people, local and military, headed for the theater to see the film *Carefree* with Ginger Rogers and Fred Astaire. Mariquita's group was followed closely by the group of young sailors, their muffled jokes and laughter directed at the four young ladies in their high-fashion outfits. Certainly, the sailors saw through the girls' pseudo-sophistication.

Gaiety Theater. (M.A.R.C. Manuscripts)

Mariquita and Carolyn waited in the lobby for the movie to start. They did not want to take a seat until Marian and Delia were through working and could sit with them. As the lights were turned down, they appeared and the girls took off their hats and headed for the balcony. In its shadowed darkness, all of the girls sat next to their current attractions, except Mariquita who sat determinedly between Marian and Delia, their boyfriends on the outside of them.

During the movie, Mariquita could feel Eddie's eyes on her and it was making her uncomfortable, but when she glanced in his direction, he was not looking. Several times she stole a glance and each time he was looking ahead, apparently enjoying the film. For some reason this disturbed Mariquita, so by the end of the movie she was not in her usual high spirits. Fortunately, she easily found Frankie in the crowded lobby waiting for her, having decided to go home with him rather than wait around for her girl friends, as they were always reluctant to leave their companions. She bade everyone a good night promising to meet her friends the following morning so they could all bicycle together to the Elks Club picnic at Tumon Bay.

Halfway home, Mariquita and her younger brother passed a couple of servicemen who apparently had drank too much at one of the bars frequented by the military.

"Hey, where are you going, pretty girl?" one of the drunken sailors asked. Ignoring him, Mariquita and Frankie hurried on. "Let me come with you. I'll show you a good time," he said, leaving the other man and starting after them.

Mariquita and Frankie walked faster as the American stumbled along behind. He soon stopped and shouted, "You dirty native! Who do you think you are?"

Hearing a commotion behind her, Mariquita looked back and in the dim light saw Eddie knock the man down. "Hurry, Frankie," she said, urging her brother on as tears filled her eyes.

3

An American in Guam

As soon as Eddie struck the man, he realized that he had over-reacted in his defense of Mariquita. He was normally a gentle person, placing reason above violence, but his infatuation with Mariquita had disrupted his equilibrium. For Eddie, life on Guam was usually peaceful and harmonious. This particular incident was highly upsetting for him because of the racial remark the other American had made to Mariquita. Shortly after joining the Navy, he became aware of the racial prejudice that existed among many of his fellow countrymen toward any non-white person, and had made comments that could be considered racist. Much of it was due to his innocence in growing up isolated on a southern Indiana farm and his interest in being accepted. Racial prejudice on Guam, although it existed, was mostly hidden and rarely vocalized in public. Most likely the drinking had brought the American's true feelings to surface.

To ensure peaceful coexistence, maintained since the American takeover of Guam, the paternalistic Naval Government was mindful of the Guamanians' feelings and kept a watchful eye on the Americans, especially the military personnel who could expect swift disciplinary action for any offensive behavior.

Keeping the peace was not difficult and strict supervision was unnecessary for two reasons. First, the Guamanians, having a propensity for harmony, were easily pleased, and when treated with consideration, remained good natured and hospitable. Second, for the most part, American military personnel exhibited exemplary character because of the high standards enlistees were required to meet. Military personnel were proud to serve their country and felt that they were personal representatives of America. Edward Neal Howard was such a person.

He was born on a cold, icy January morning in 1920 on a forty-acre farm near Carlisle, Indiana. An elderly neighbor woman took a look at the newborn baby and said, "He has a high brow, and is destined to eat his bread in foreign lands." His parents, Levada Ellen Neal and Mervin Christopher Howard, were amused but of course did not take the prophecy seriously.

Growing up in the country was good, and young Edward, of English, Irish and Scottish descent, grew tall and strong. Besides working on the farm, he sometimes made trips to Terre Haute, a city he found fascinating, trucking melons and other produce to the Farmers' Market. Most of his leisure time was spent reading.

Edward's mother occasionally worked as a substitute teacher, and she encouraged her exceptionally bright son to study. He would go to the town library weekly and check out as many books as he was allowed. Through his reading he gained knowledge of the world and excelled in his academic studies. He also learned to play the trumpet.

Reading became an obsession for Edward, and out of it came a growing desire for travel and adventure. When he graduated from high school at the age of sixteen, having skipped a grade, he left the farm, turning down a scholarship to a university. For almost a year, this well-read, handsome, intelligent farm boy lived the life of a hobo, riding freight trains and bumming rides. He worked as a ranch hand and dishwasher among other jobs, and stayed in hobo jungles and skid row missions. Then one day in San Pedro, California, he watched the Navy's Pacific Fleet sail in from Hawaii. What a sight! He saw it as his passage to travel and adventure.

Returning immediately to Indiana, he joined the U.S. Navy as a band member. But soon after his enlistment, he discovered that bands didn't travel much, so he transferred to engineering, and attended machinist school in Norfolk, Virginia.

In December 1938 at the age of eighteen, he was on the transport ship *USS Henderson* headed for the island of Guam where he was assigned for a tour of duty. As he watched the shoreline of the United States recede into the distance, he anticipated the adventure waiting for him on a tiny island over 5,000 miles away. He was happy that his request for overseas duty had been approved. It would be seven years before he would see that shoreline again, seven years that would seem a lifetime.

Toward the end of the second week at sea, after a brief stop in Hawaii, Edward saw Guam for the first time. Excited and restless, he arose before reveille. In the predawn he stood alone against the railing and inhaled the fresh salt air. The movement of the ship gliding through the water was the only sound he heard on an otherwise silent ocean. The first break of light shined on land in the distance, rising jade green out of the deep blue of the Pacific, and he said to himself, "At last, my adventure – the island of Guam."

All that he knew about the island was what he had found in an encyclopedia.

> *Guam is a tropical island thirty miles long and an average of seven miles wide in the Pacific Ocean north of the equator and west of the International Date Line. It is the largest and southernmost of the Mariana Islands, a part of Micronesia. The discovery of the island by the Western world has been attributed to Magellan who visited Guam in 1521 on the first expedition to sail around the world. The island has a varied landscape ranging from the high limestone plateau in the north to the volcanic hills and lush vegetation in the south. It is encircled by a fringing coral reef and peopled by natives thought to have originated in Southeast Asia.*

On his arrival, Edward was assigned to the *USS Penguin*, an old minesweeper that looked like a large seagoing tug. Its number was

AM33 and had been com-
missioned in 1918. During
the 1920s, the *Penguin* served
as a gunboat on the Yangtze
River in China. She was 187
feet long, 35 feet wide, and
had a crew of forty-five enlisted men and one officer.
Besides offshore patrol duty,
the ship was used to trans-

Edward Neal Howard on the USS Penguin.
(Perez Howard Photo Collection)

port supplies to the southern villages and to carry the governor, a
captain in the U.S. Navy, on his yearly inspection trips.

When Edward arrived, there were 22,000 Guamanians and
around 600 Americans on the island. Nearly all the Americans were
military personnel and their dependents. Other than the government
buildings in Agana, most of the military installations were located
around Apra Harbor, especially on Orote Point near the town of Sumay, the second largest community on the island. In addition to the
military facilities on Orote Point, the Pan American World Airways,
the Pacific Commercial Cable Company, and the Standard Oil storage
plant buildings were also located there.

USS Penguin
Guam, M.I.
December 17, 1938

Dear Mother and Dad,

At last I arrived at my new home and the first appearance is
very pleasing to the eye. The trip from Honolulu was without
excitement whatsoever. We arrived here around 8:00 a.m.,
Friday. They transferred us around 10:00 a.m. and you can
bet I was rather glad to get off the Henderson – "Misery barge"
they call it.

The island is not so very pretty from a distance of about a mile or inside the harbor. By the way, the harbor is a natural one and has a breakwater of coral reef. One of the prettiest sights I have seen is the breakers as they roll over it, real blue with white caps.

When we go ashore the boat takes us up a narrow channel about a half mile long to the dock at Piti which is merely a landing. A couple of beer joints and a small food store comprise the business section but the houses are thick from there to Agana, the capital about 4 miles away (pop. 8,000). The houses are of boards, a lot with thatched roofs, the better class having screens, others nothing. The drawback about going to Agana is that it costs 75 cents taxi fare, or if three or more, then 25 cents each. After I get my fine and debts paid around next June, I'll get a contract for about $5 where you can ride a roundtrip to Agana every day for 30 days.

For amusement there are pool halls, a theatre, a dance about once a week. The native girls are prettier than I expected and some are beauties. More about them at some future writing.

It is not very hot here, in fact, I find it cool. A rain can come without any warning, though, even with the sun shining.

There is a crew on here of about 50 men. And what do we do – two things as far as work is concerned – stand 6 hour watch every 36 hours (fireroom) and overhaul the boiler when it has 1,000 steaming hours on it. Regulations – none. Go ashore in civilian clothes or swimming trunks. Eat like an officer. Plenty of golden colored butter, etc. Have good bunks and lockers. Nobody ever sweeps down the compartments, though. We have a phonograph (about worn out) and about 30 late records. Can get natives to do our laundry for $4 a month.

We (in the fireroom) have a native (goo-goo) to do all our work for us. He shines bridgework, cleans floor-plates, and dries bilges for a dollar a piece each pay. Around $14 dollars a month. Some life, eh? Liberty from 12:30 to midnight, overnight if we want it, but no servicemen are allowed on streets after 12:30 a.m.

There are a swell bunch of men on here. It will probably be the easiest tour of duty I will ever have.

Hereafter I will send an airmail letter about once every two weeks. There isn't much to write anyhow.

Our next trip is to Manila about June. Be sure to send the papers and magazines.

With love,
Edward

Every other day, Eddie, as friends called him, was off duty and spent the time exploring the island and seeing what the city had to offer. He became close friends with shipmates Joseph Hanzek and John Zahnen. They would go ashore together, most often to the enlisted men's service club where they bowled, played cards and relaxed. Eddie was amazed that the island was so civilized. He found that just about anything that anyone needed was available in the stores in Agana. The only adjustment he had to make was to the slow pace of island life. Within a short period of time he fell in love with the island and would love it even more after he got to know Mariquita.

He could not believe his eyes when he first saw her. She was the prettiest girl he had ever seen. She conversed easily, and he was dazzled by her smile. As he became acquainted with her, he found her to be a bit of a pixie, with a sharp mind and sense of humor, and very feminine. Another thing that attracted him was her outspokenness in advocating Chamorro equality. He found it admirable. He was made aware of this aspect of her when he read an interview with her that appeared in *Collier's Magazine*, a popular American magazine. The article, "Guam Haunted Paradise" by W.B. Courtney, had made Mariquita somewhat of a celebrity on the island. In the April 18, 1939 issue, Courtney described Mariquita as "small, dainty, lusciously pretty with melted licorice eyes," and Eddie was in full agreement with the author's view. Courtney wrote:

> *There is a school in Agana built and supported by special taxes levied on the Navy personnel, cigarettes and luxuries at the commissary, with a per head charge of $1.50 monthly for officers' children and $1.00 for enlisted men's. This is called the American school. "What do they mean by that name?" demands Mariquita. "Aren't all schools in Guam American schools? Don't we salute the same flag, sing the same patriotic hymns in our classrooms, love and respect the same great men? I know they pay especially for it while our children go free but don't you think it is a very tactless name?"*

> *You would be constitutionally unable to disagree with anything Mariquita says, and she likes that and tells you more about Guam schools. All children wear simple uniforms of the very cheapest material, which is supposed to knock out inferiority complexes. Education is compulsory between seven and twelve. Limited accommodations make it necessary to have competitive examinations for admission to the junior-senior George Washington High School. "Only lately," says Mariquita significantly, "have civics been taught. I guess they didn't want us asking too many questions about citizenship." All teachers were United States Marines and the results were not as unorthodox as you might have feared. You are struck by one fact. The instant school lets out all kids, even of the highest grades, lapse into Chamorro,*

When Eddie began talking to Mariquita, she seemed to enjoy their conversations. What recently happened to cause her to change, he did not know, but all of a sudden, she seemed cold and conversations with her were difficult. But he was too far gone to give up. He was enamored with her. She was in his everyday thoughts, dreams and fantasies. He was determined to win her over.

Determined or not, Eddie was not making much progress until fate, in one of its surprising moves, dealt him a trump card which opened Mariquita's heart – an opportunity to show his concern for her welfare.

The day after Eddie struck the other serviceman, Mariquita looked at him differently as he approached her on the beach, where she was sitting with her girlfriends, tired after having bicycled from Agana.

"Hey, sailor, I think you left your shirt on!" Mariquita exclaimed, immediately wishing she hadn't made such a silly remark, especially in front of her friends, who looked at her strangely.

Eddie looked down, quickly realizing what she meant, and smiled. Days in the hot sun had tanned his skin except where his undershirt had been.

Mariquita, embarrassed by what she had said, barely managed an audible, "How are you Eddie?"

"Fine," he replied. "And you?"

"Fine, thanks."

"Can I help you take your things to the shelter?"

"Sure, if you would like to."

Mariquita and the girls got up and began unpacking their fully loaded bicycle baskets and soon they were on their way to the picnic shelter. Elks Club members, family and friends and a number of military personnel were there. They were all having a good time barbecuing, swimming and enjoying each other's company, a spirited game of volleyball drawing a big crowd nearby. Walking on ahead, the others left Mariquita and Eddie alone.

"Eddie, I want to thank you for last night," Mariquita said, as they followed behind the girls. "It was nothing, Mariquita. I only wish it hadn't happened. I hope it didn't give you a bad impression of us."

"Of course not. What is one drunken sailor?"

"He wasn't a sailor," Eddie stated. "He was a Marine."

"Oh, Eddie," Mariquita laughed. "Is there that much of a difference?"

"You bet," he answered with a grin.

That day at the beach was the beginning of their eventual union. Even when apart, they felt together. Looking up from helping get the food ready, Mariquita would catch Eddie looking her way. He, in turn, while playing volleyball could sense her on the sidelines urging him on.

Later that afternoon they sat apart from the others, mesmerized by their newfound friendship and the sparkle of romance, plying each other with curious questions about their lives. When the girls called Mariquita to leave, it was like a rude awakening from a beautiful dream she was having. Marian, after hearing Eddie express the desire to bicycle back to Agana, gave him her bicycle, opting to ride in her brother's car, and the dream-like day continued as Mariquita and Eddie pedaled behind Delia and Carolyn along the tropical country road into the city.

The days passed quickly and their romance grew.

"Mariquita, I don't understand you," Marian said one day as they were sitting in Mayhew's Ice Cream Shop. "First you didn't like Eddie, and now you want to be with him all the time."

"I didn't say I didn't like him. I just ... I don't know, maybe I sensed something and was afraid."

"Well, you're certainly not acting like you're afraid now. I think everyone in Agana knows about you two. Only this morning, Mother was saying how you two were always together."

"But you know we are never alone, Marian."

"Yes, but people talk. I think you should tell your parents before they find out. You know how people gossip."

"I don't know. Ever since Papa quit working at the school and joined the Navy's Insular Force to work at the Navy Yard in Piti, he's not so keen on American servicemen. Did I tell you that Eddie met him?"

"No! Really? Did Eddie say anything?"

"Thank goodness, no."

"Well, I think you'd better tell your father, at least. You can't just let things go on the way they are."

"Maybe ... I've got to go now. I wish it would stop raining. It's been raining for almost an hour. Oh, I'll just have to get wet."

"Here, take my umbrella. I'm so close to home."

"Thanks, Marian. I'll drop it off after class tonight. You know, Marian, I really love you."

"Oh, Mariquita, get going before I take the umbrella back!"

The friendship between Mariquita and Eddie continued to blossom and Mariquita continued to keep it a secret from her parents. At the beginning, it would have been premature to tell them because that would be asking them to accept him into the family, a serious step, especially since he was an American, a step she was not yet ready to take. Totally lost in the rapture of romantic love, she had been content to remain there, not wanting to face making the choice between her girlish freedom and the necessary womanly commitment. Now, however, the situation demanded that she face this problem. Using her father as an excuse was only one of several excuses she had to justify her inaction.

That evening after class, Mariquita found Eddie waiting for her as he had done on his days off for the past month. Respecting her wishes, he would walk her only part of the way home, then leave to join friends. They walked along together in silence. Mariquita felt that something was on Eddie's mind, so she waited for him to speak.

"You know, Mariquita, we are never alone together. We're always around other people. Don't you ever want to be with just me.?"

"We're alone now, Eddie. Why do we need to be alone anyway?" she teased.

"I would like to be free to talk to you."

"Eddie, you are free to talk now. What do you want to say?"

"Mariquita, can't you be serious? Don't you understand?"

"Yes, yes, I understand. I just don't want to talk about it. This is the way things have to be. We've talked about it before. Please be patient."

Neither of them at ease in disharmony, they ended the conversation and became lost in their own thoughts. Eddie had had the usual school crushes, but his experience with girls was limited, and he was perplexed about how to achieve a more intimate relationship with Mariquita. It was not sex he was thinking about, but simply a more satisfactory way of expressing his love. Holding hands in the theater surrounded by friends and kissing on the sly were not enough for his romantic nature. He did not want to have to be constantly aware of others, and it frustrated him that he could not even touch her when they were walking down the street. For Eddie, this secrecy was taking the pleasure out of the romance and making it seem wrong.

Mariquita knew she had to do something. She had waited too long to act and now she was making Eddie unhappy. She understood Eddie's feelings for recently she too had felt discontented with the state of their relationship. But it was only now that she was motivated to do something about it.

When they reached the front door of the theater, Mariquita spoke. "Wait here, Eddie. I have to drop off Marian's umbrella. Then, will you walk me the rest of the way home?"

Surprised, Eddie said, "Are you sure it will be all right?"

"Yes, don't worry. Just wait here a moment." Mariquita returned shortly, grabbed Eddie's hand, and they walked hand in hand towards her home.

Nights in Guam have a special attraction all their own. The sky, in its solitary vastness, dominates the landscape, and even when there is no moon, the stars radiate a special light, a brilliance seen only in the tropics. Torches held that night by fishermen dotted the reef, and in the city, the serene houses emitted warm glows in the dusky darkness. The quietness was so remarkable that it was almost audible, and the muffled Chamorro voices, the ebb and tide of the surf, and other night sounds were more an accompaniment than an intrusion.

In front of her home, Mariquita faced Eddie, took hold of both his hands and held them. He leaned down and kissed her tenderly; she had to stand on her tiptoes to return his kiss.

"I love you, Mariquita," he said.

"I love you too, Eddie," she whispered as they parted.

She held onto Eddie's words as she entered the house and went into the kitchen. Da was there ironing, the scent from the slow burning coconut shells in the iron filled the room like incense.

"Auntie Da, I am going to marry an American," Mariquita announced breathlessly.

Grinning, Da lifted her head and said, "*Hu tungo' ha*," Mariquita threw her arms around her saying, "I should have known I couldn't keep a secret from you!"

Not long afterwards, Eddie met Mariquita's family and was introduced to their way of life. Although they were a modern Guamanian family, they were still very much Chamorro in how they lived. He was impressed by their courtesy, which extended to their speaking only English in his presence. Moreover, they pleased him by always speaking patriotically about America. Problems he had anticipated did not arise. He did notice a certain reserve in their conversations with him, but he believed that familiarity would remove it. In the meantime, he would endeavor to gain their respect and learn everything he could about their culture. To Mariquita and Eddie, the lifting of the shroud of secrecy on their friendship was like opening a new book and seeing another world.

After gaining permission from Papa and Mama Pai, they were now dating openly and the tension that existed between them vanished. Every other day, Eddie would see Mariquita after she got off work and since she had finished night school, they had the evenings free. They continued to see their friends and go to the movies, plaza concerts, ball games and other activities. But most of the time it was clear that they were together, even though they were always chaperoned, usually by one of Mariquita's brothers.

The next time the *Penquin* went to the southern village of Umatac for the annual Magellan's Day celebrations, Mariquita was among the citizens aboard. Eddie attended family fiestas, in time becoming acquainted with her relatives: the Taijerons, the Aguons, the Unpingcos, the Perezes, and the Torreses. He went fishing in the family's outrigger canoe with the boys, visited the ranch with Papa and Pepe, and had many delightful conversations with Mama Pai, whom he considered a jewel of a woman. He also tried to learn Chamorro, but when he tried out a few words on Auntie Da, it produced peals of laughter. In gratitude for their generosity, he occasionally brought gifts, such as coffee, sugar, canned goods, Navy biscuits, and toiletries from the Navy commissary.

One evening, Papa asked Eddie point blank what his intentions were regarding his daughter. He knew that half of Eddie's two-year tour of duty was over, and he was worried for both of them. Not long afterwards, Eddie, after dinner at the Perez house, asked Mariquita to take a walk down the beach because he wanted to talk to her privately. It was a beautiful, starry night, the moon bright enough to see the coconut trees silhouetted against the sky. They walked to an outcropping of rocks and sat down. After a few light kisses, Eddie reached into his pocket and took out a small box. He opened it, removed an engagement ring and said, "You've known for some time how much I love you and want to marry you. Will you marry me?" Just as Mariquita replied, "Yes," they heard a commotion. Turning, they saw Frankie running to the house, apparently to tell his parents.

Eddie's parents in Indiana had known for some time about their son's infatuation with Mariquita, so it was not supprising when he informed them that he wanted to marry her. At first, they were against it expressing concerns similar to those of Mariquita's parents about them being too young and about marrying a foreigner. But in the end, they consented and gave him their blessing.

Since their romance had taken off, Mariquita spent less and less time with her girlfriends. Besides the time she spent with Eddie, she was becoming more involved with community organizations. She and Mama Pai helped to organize the Ladies' Auxiliary of the Fleet Reserve Association. Mariquita became the secretary and Mama the chaplain. Her detachment from the group of girlfriends altered it somewhat, as they were all beginning to go their separate ways. Marian was already scheduled to go to the Philippines to study beauty culture. Despite the different directions they were taking, nothing would disrupt their close bonds as much as marriage would. They voiced their sorrow at the thought of losing Mariquita, saying that she was too young to get married, especially since she had such a bright future ahead of her, and pointed out that there were so many things left for them to do together. Mariquita, having decided that her future was to be with Eddie, was not the least bit swayed.

Reluctant at first to accept it, the girls then rallied around her, convinced of her sincerity and noting the marked change in her behavior. She was more mature now, content with her new role; the fire within her apparently contained by love – a love that would be severely tested.

4

A Marriage of Cultures

Throughout the Catholic world, the eighth of December is celebrated as the feast of the Immaculate Conception of the Blessed Virgin Mary. In 1939 on Guam, a procession of over 3,000 people, all dressed in their finest, began at 5:00 p.m. at the Dulce Nombre de Maria Cathedral adjacent to the Plaza in Agana and passed through the streets of the city in celebration. The statue of the Blessed Virgin Mary was mounted on a cart beautifully decorated with palm branches and flowers drawn by several

Dulce Nombre de Maria Cathedral, 1937.
(M.A.R.C. Photo Collection)

young men and accompanied by maids of honor dressed in white. The parochial school choir and the Catholic band led the procession.

With foreign eyes, Eddie watched this solemn spectacle in reverence. He was a Protestant, but he respected the religion of others. Watching Mariquita and members of her family pass by, he thought how nice it was that their religious differences had not presented any difficulties. He and Mariquita had often talked about it, coming to the realization that they both believed in the basic teachings of the Bible, and in other areas, they were willing to compromise.

The Christmas holidays marked the beginning of Eddie's second year on Guam. One of the things he and Mariquita did was attend the "smoker" sponsored by the Guam Teachers' Association, a charitable event featuring boxing matches and entertainment. American boxer Jack Dempsey was the guest of honor and refereed the main bout.

Eddie spent Christmas day with the family. In the morning, the children took baskets of food and other gifts to relatives and friends. At noon, there was a feast of roast pig, chicken, *escabeche*, taro and yams. Later, a number of women and their daughters, paying religious homage, came to the house carrying a small statue of the Christ Child, and in the early evening the family held their *Nubenan Niñu* (nine days of prayer for the Christ Child).

All during the day, people came to the house. By late evening, there was quite a gathering, and a party began with plenty of food, betelnut and tuba. There was harmonica and guitar playing, singing and dancing, Spanish card games and storytelling. Eddie joined in the festivities, an accepted member of the family. The day ended with the midnight mass.

Toward the end of the year, Mariquita and Eddie applied to the Naval authorities for permission to marry, as U.S. policy required all service personnel to obtain permission to marry a non-American. At that time, in spite of their loyalty and patriotism, Guamanians were not classified as Americans, a fact which upset Mariquita and was often a topic of conversation. They were married by the Reverend Adelbert Donlon in a quiet ceremony in the parish house of the Cathedral.

For several weeks, the young couple stayed with Mariquita's family until their rented house was ready for occupancy. Eddie was not too happy about this since the rented house had all the things he considered necessary and he was anxious to begin their married life together. But Mama Pai and Papa insisted that they stay with them until the house was in perfect order. The furniture that Papa had made for them had to be finished, the house had to be properly cleaned and painted inside and out and the yard beautified. The whole family was often at the house putting the place in order, the days ending with a party. It was during his stay with Mariquita's family that Eddie began calling Mariquita "Tippy," an endearment she loved, in reference to her having to stand on her tiptoes to kiss him.

Mariquita and Edward.
(Perez Howard Photo Collection)

The house was in Tepungan, an area near Piti, not far from Apra Harbor where the *Penguin* was anchored. It was a small, wood-framed house with a large, screened porch, nestled near neighboring houses with the verdant jungle and steep hills behind it, and the ocean across the road.

Happy to be in her new role as a young housewife, Mariquita quit her job, devoting her time to making a dream life for the two of them. She sewed curtains and bedspreads, arranged the furniture and decorated the rooms, planned and cooked gourmet Guamanian-American meals and kept the house so clean it put Eddie's "spic-and-span" ship to shame. She found that Eddie was easy to cook for, his favorite meal being "Guamanian hamburger" and rice.

When they went into the city, they visited Mariquita's family and saw old friends. Their social life now also included married couples, particularly Eddie's shipmates who were also married to Guamanians. They visited John Zahnen, his friend who had also recently married, and the Chief Boatswain's Mate Robert O'Brien, who lived nearby. They enjoyed seeing his extensive seashell collection. But mostly, they were content to spend their time at home. Mariquita shared Eddie's love for books and they enjoyed discussing everything from the books they read to the social and political aspects of the island. Their marriage was a happy one, and it would be further strengthened by the birth of their baby on September 17, 1940 at the Susana Hospital in Agana.

Guam, M.I.
September 20, 1940

Dear Mother and Dad,

A big change has taken place in my life now, for I have a fine baby boy. He was born around 1:30 a.m., Sept. 17, which was Tuesday morning here. He weighed 8 lbs. 3½ ounces at birth and is very healthy. He doesn't cry much except when he is real hungry. He drinks around 1½-to-2 ounces of milk every 4 hours. He has a "pug" nose like his mother and I think to her goes the greatest resemblance. His complexion seems normal and he is very rosy cheeked.

The only name he has so far is the nickname "Atlas" which I gave him because of his size. As it is a boy, she has the privilege of naming him. If it had been a girl, I would have chosen the name. She wants to wait for your letter before deciding on it.

As I was ashore this last Sunday, I got permission and stayed over until noon Thursday. At 3:00 a.m. Sunday night (or rather Monday morn) she woke me up that she was having pains like a stomachache about every 15 min. At 0800, I took her over to the hospital. From there on she did not have much rest. She is coming along fine now.

She is in a private room, clean and with good furnishings. Cost me $2.25 a day which covers everything. Through the influence of her mother, instead of having a normal staff of one doctor and nurses, she had the two best doctors in the hospital present. Her mother also is hiring a special nurse for her. And the many things they have given us for the baby! So many people have called or sent flowers. Mariquita said they were talking about putting money in the bank for him.

Mariquita named her son Chris Allen Howard, and soon after his birth, they moved into a larger house in Agana to have more room and to be closer to Mariquita's family. In addition to their son, they also had one of Mariquita's cousins living with them to help take care of the household.

Moving to Agana meant that Eddie had to take the bus to his ship, but he didn't mind as he had learned to enjoy riding the open bus when he and Mariquita used to take it to town when they lived in Tepungan. The ride gave him time to think about his good fortune in having a fine family and a wonderful life. Chris was a healthy baby, a perfect mixture of the two of them, and a joy to his parents. They had him baptized in the Catholic faith with his godparents, Concepcion P. Torres and Edmund Okada in attendance.

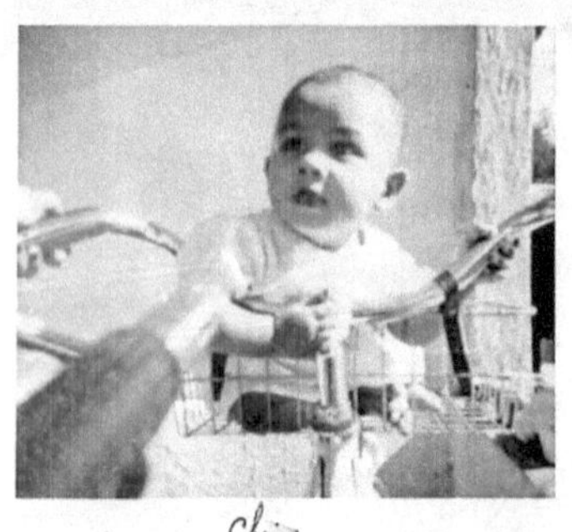
Baby Chris. (Perez Howard Photo Collection)

In their married life, Mariquita and Eddie continued to become Americanized and Chamorroized, each wanting to be that much closer to the other. One day, while reading the *Guam Recorder*, a monthly publication of the Naval government, Eddie became very upset and read part of it to Mariquita.

*is excellent and undoubtedly all of us are united in speeding the
day when in thoughts, language and ideals the people of this
lovely island are thoroughly Americanized and may truly enjoy
the benefits of an American form of government. It is a fact that
inasmuch as the United States governs here, the Chamorro
people should make a determined effort to throw off the last
remnants of customs, languages and ideas to which they cannot
be sentimentally attached as a relic of their former government
by another nation. To assist in this process is the duty of every
American on the island.*

Although Mariquita was bothered by the editorial, she was not
sure why Eddie was so upset. She wanted to become a true American,
not thinking what it truly meant to "throw off" her people's customs
and language. Wasn't it better to be American?

Eddie became more agitated as he tried to explain his feelings
about the editorial and the need for Mariquita to maintain pride in
her own culture. Because of Eddie's angry tone, Mariquita paid little
attention to what he was saying. She nodded her head, but hurt, she
retreated into herself where she remained until the following evening
when Eddie apologized.

"Tippy, I'm sorry about last night. I guess I just got a little excited.
This total Americanization campaign bothers me. It's wrong."

"I forgive you Eddie, but you didn't have to get upset with me."

"I'm really sorry, honey," Eddie said, as he got up from the kitchen
table and went over and kissed her. "I could never be mad at you."

"Eddie, I read the article again and now I don't like it either. It
makes me feel that it's bad to be Chamorro," Mariquita said, as Eddie
pulled up a chair and sat next to her.

"That's what made me mad. Telling you to get rid of your culture
is wrong. No matter how Americanized you become, you will always
be a Chamorro and you need your culture for your own identity."

"I'm surprised, Eddie, that you feel so strongly about it."

"Tippy, when I fell in love and married you, I also loved and married your culture and I don't want you to lose it. It certainly is confusing and mixed up, but it's still your culture and it's a beautiful one. You don't have to give up your identity to be an American."

"Eddie, you're so wonderful! That's why I love you. I want to be the best American and the proudest Chamorro."

"You're crazy."

"I know. Now, about your drinking."

"I wondered when that would come up."

It was not that Eddie was a heavy drinker, but that drinking marred Mariquita's vision of the perfect Christian family life. Knowing this and wanting to please her, Eddie started drinking less. As time went on, they began reading the Bible together and their life began to grow spiritually. To please Eddie, Mariquita would sometimes go with him to a Protestant church service. Attending, she never felt she was abandoning her own church, but that she was expanding her faith in God by accompanying her husband. It was not long before Eddie stopped drinking. This pleased Mariquita and now she felt that their life was truly perfect.

And a good one it was. Aside from their love for one another, they were in good financial shape. Despite the modest wages of a sailor, Eddie's income was more than most Guamanians. At that time, even

Edward and Mariquita enjoy becoming new parents. (Perez Howard Photo Collection)

if a Guamanian did the same job as an American, the Guamanian was often paid only half of what the American was earning. In a system where money is the criterion for social status, this inequitable wage scale created an upper class of wealthy Guamanians and military personnel and their dependents. The Howard family, therefore, were in a high social position, in part, because of their American connection. And since Mariquita was from a prominent Guamanian family, their social standing was further strengthened and made the future look very good indeed.

Everything was going well when on November 3, 1940, one of the strongest typhoons since 1918 struck the island. Although Guam was on the edge of the typhoon belt, there had not been a serious storm in recent years. Everyone began typhoon preparations - more out of habit than a feeling of impending danger - after being warned that one was heading their way. Having been off duty and ashore, Eddie was called back to his ship. Before he left, he helped Mariquita secure the house and then took her and the baby to the Perez's home, since their house was structurally sounder.

In the harbor, the *Penguin* was safely anchored and attached to a buoy as Eddie and the others who had been ashore approached her in a small motor launch. They boarded the ship and helped the rest of the crew batten down the hatches and secure the ship for the storm.

As night fell, the winds accelerated and the rains came. Unrelenting, it continued throughout the night, the sea sporadically tossing the ship. Leaks developed above the sleeping compartments and water came down the ventilators. The water, mixed with fuel oil seeping from tanks along the bottom of the ship, sloshed around the inside decks and up the bulkheads. By morning, the ship, though still moored to the buoy, was bobbing maniacally in the water. The main engine and the rudder had to be used to keep her headed to the buoy. By noon, the typhoon was at its peak with winds well over 150 miles per hour. Both of the *Penguin*'s life rafts were smashed, and the port boiler room ventilator was ripped off.

Below deck, Eddie and the rest of the boiler room crew were having a rough time keeping steam up. Earlier, looking out a porthole before going down to the boiler room, Eddie had seen waves higher than the ship, washing even the small, round windows on the main deck with ugly blue-brown colored water. He was worried about his family, but his immediate concern was the ship and the lives of those aboard. That afternoon, the worst of the storm had passed and the wind and rain slowly began to abate. The next morning as he looked out and saw the disheveled shoreline and the debris floating in the harbor, Eddie became anxious about his family.

Mariquita's family had prepared for the storm, but there was no way they could have prepared for the magnitude of it. The older family members spent most of the night awake as the winds pounded the house. Waves were lapping at the back door, and the outside kitchen had already been sent crashing into the sea. Wet sand and a variety of flying objects pelted the house. At Mama Pai's urging, they decided to leave their house and go to the Ada's, Delia's parents' home, which was not far from them, but was farther away from the ocean. Everyone was ready by 4 a.m. when the typhoon whistle blew again and a second red light was lit on the power plant smoke stack, signaling typhoon condition two and worse winds to come.

In the debris-filled street in the eerie morning darkness, Mariquita held her month-old baby protectively to her breast, bundled in Eddie's Navy blanket and poncho as the wind and rain beat down on her and her family. Slowly, they made their way through the streets to the Ada's, arriving wet and frightened, but safe.

A few hours later, the full force of the typhoon ripped through the city. The first to go were frail houses along the ocean. Sheets of metal roofing went flying, trees were uprooted, and telephone and power lines went down.

The following day, when Eddie made his way into the city along the almost impassable road, he was aghast at the devastation and nearly frantic about his family. Trees that he once saw at their loveliest were now nude and broken, and he could not help but think how everything had been so wonderful just a few days ago. "Oh, dear God," he prayed, "please make everything all right."

Typhoon damage in Agana. (M.A.R.C. Photo Collection)

Mariquita was in the yard of her family's house helping, as best she could, to clear up the debris when Eddie arrived. She looked up, and upon seeing him, ran to embrace him.

"Eddie, Eddie, thank God! I was so worried about you. We heard the ship was all right but when you didn't come home ... I wanted to go look for you, but Mama said wait..." Mariquita sobbed, clinging to him.

"There, there, Tippy, everything is fine now. I was so worried about you, too. How is everyone?"

"Everybody is fine, including Chris, but we had to leave and stay at the Ada's. It was so frightening, Eddie!" Gradually, as he continued to hold her, Mariquita stopped trembling. "Have you been to our house?" Eddie asked.

"Yes, the roof leaked and a corner of the house was damaged, but nothing too bad. Oh, yes, remember the front steps you made? Well, they're gone. I couldn't find them anywhere."

Eddie laughed. "Well, I guess if that's all that is missing, we're lucky. How's everything here?"

"Some of the roof got torn off, but they're fixing it now. And water came into the house, so we had to clean that up. You can see what a mess the yard is. But I guess we are lucky, some people lost everything."

"Let me say hello to your parents, then let's go home. I love you, Tippy."

"No more than I do you, Eddie," she said, smiling, as they walked to the house.

Mariquita and Chris.
(Perez Howard Photo Collection)

For months afterwards, military personnel and the people worked hand in hand cleaning up the debris and repairing the damage wrought by the typhoon. Working together for the common good in the aftermath of destruction brought about a certain amity and all shared the camaraderie. Although it would be a long time before the island fully recovered, especially agriculturally, there was no despondency and daily life soon returned to normal.

The months passed and it was almost Chris' first birthday. He was a good child, who rarely fussed, and the contentment in his dark eyes reflected all the love he was given. The happiness he gave Mariquita was such that she seldom left him.

Happiness had always been a part of Mariquita's life, but marriage to Eddie and motherhood expanded it in many new and delightful ways. She could not think of asking for more. With each new day, her love for Eddie and Chris grew.

Proud of her family, she enjoyed the walks she and Eddie took with Chris in his stroller dressed in one of her hand-sewn creations. Once, they even took him to her favorite spot on Tutuhan Hill. Eddie had found that walk tiring as he had to push the stroller up the hill, but he would not even let Mariquita help, as she was in the sixth month of her second pregnancy. He hadn't even wanted Mariquita to make the climb, but gave in when she said it would be good luck for the coming baby. How could he argue with that?

As much as they enjoyed just being together, they still remained close to their friends and often entertained them at home. John Zahnen had recently been transferred to the States, and they were sorry to see him leave. Marian, since returning from the Philippines, was now working as a beautician and was engaged to Robert White, the young officer on the *Penguin*.

The girls still got together, and still kept up with the latest fashions. What was happening outside their immediate world, however, was usually overlooked unless it had a direct bearing on their lives. In recent weeks, there had been more talk about the tense situation between the United States and Japan. This did have an effect on their lives when the Mayhews decided it was best to leave Guam. Carolyn was unhappy about having to leave her friends, but going to America had always been one of her dreams.

"I promise to write, Mariquita, and I'll send you all the new magazines," Carolyn assured her.

"It's going to be so different without you, and I have a feeling that you'll never come back," Mariquita said sadly.

"It's more of a visit than anything permanent. Of course, I'll come back! Who knows, maybe I'll meet someone and come back with a husband!"

"Eddie will be transferred back to the States before too long. Then I'll get to meet his parents. If you're not back by then, maybe we will just come to see you. Carolyn, I'm going to miss you so much."

One last time, the four friends got together before Carolyn's departure. They talked and talked about their times together, about the future and about how all of them would eventually be married, live close to one another, and life would go dreamingly on.

Soon after the Mayhews left, the government ordered the evacuation of all the American dependents, but not the Guamanian dependents of Americans. The American dependents left on October 17, 1941, and what a sad day it was for those leaving and for the many friends and loved ones staying behind. Everyone thought it an unnecessary precaution. Japan wouldn't dare attack the United States, and besides, negotiations were being conducted.

Life went on, and the only concern Mariquita and Eddie had was the imminent birth of their second child.

5
Invasion

MARIQUITA HAD BEEN AWAKE for some time. After a trip to the washroom she lay peacefully on the clean white sheets of the hospital bed waiting for the nurse to bring her nine-day old daughter.

She had awakened long before the first sound of the Cathedral bells that called the people to early Mass. It was Monday, December 8, 1941, and the feast of the Immaculate Conception of the Blessed Virgin Mary. Time had passed quickly since Mariquita and Eddie had celebrated their first feast day together two years prior and this would be the first time she would not be an active participant in the festivities.

As if hypnotized, Mariquita stared at the beaded slippers on the floor next to her bed. Her mother had given them to her when she entered the hospital. The early rays of sunlight through the screened, louvered window fell upon the brightly colored beads causing them to sparkle.

She thought of Eddie. What a wonderful and handsome husband he was, and so smart. He was on his ship, but later that day he would visit her and the baby before joining the family for a picnic on her Uncle Jose Unpingco's property overlooking Tumon Bay. She wished she could be with them.

"Oh, well," she thought, "I'll be out of the hospital in another day or two." A Navy hospital corpsman entered her room and turned on the lights. His name was Tony Iannarelli, a nice young man who had helped care for Eddie last year when he was in the hospital with dengue fever. Tony was also from Indiana.

"Mrs. Howard," he addressed her, "the nurse will soon be bringing your baby to you," and he hurried off.

"That's strange," Mariquita thought, sitting up. "He didn't even say good morning. That's not like him."

From her room, Mariquita could now hear others begin to move about. Then she heard the ward doors swing open down the hall and her daughter's faint cries of hunger approaching. "My little Helen," she murmured, "you shouldn't be so hungry. Mama fed you not too long ago." She opened her hospital gown and took the baby to her breast, saying softly, "Mommy loves you." Helen sucked greedily. The chubby, dark-haired baby whimpered, then became busily content. Mariquita looked up at the nurse by her bedside, noticing a strange look on her face.

"What's this Nurse Margaret? First, Tony didn't even say good morning, and now you have sadness on your face. Is something wrong?"

"Mariquita, I shouldn't say anything and I don't want to alarm you, but since you are a Navy wife, I think you should know. We've just been informed that the Japanese have bombed Pearl Harbor."

"Oh, no! Are you sure? What are we going to do?"

"That's all the information I have now. We'll just have to wait and see. I'll let you know as soon as I hear anything else. Right now, just try to remain calm. And please, keep it quiet." She started to leave.

"Wait!" Mariquita said excitedly, and then lowering her voice asked, "How do you know this? Will they come here?"

"Mariquita, I've told you all I know. One of the Governor's men came and told us and then we heard it a little while ago on the short-wave radio. You must try and remain calm. I'll tell you if I hear anything else." She then hurried away.

"How could anything like this happen?" Mariquita wondered.

"They're still trying to work things out in Washington. This means we are going to be at war. Oh, Eddie, will you have to go?"

Mariquita looked down at her little baby and hugged her protectively. The tiny infant responded by renewing her interest in feeding. Suddenly the ward filled with noise and Mariquita could hear people running and shouting outside. Nurse Margaret came rushing into the room, almost knocking down the cart near her bed.

"Mariquita," she said sharply, "you have to leave! Quick, take the baby with you! They have just bombed Sumay and there's fear that Agana will be next! Leave the city!"

Frantically, Mariquita pushed the baby away from her, jumped out of bed, pulled out some clothes from her suitcase, and put them on. She picked up the now crying baby, grabbed the suitcase in her free hand, and fled the hospital.

The streets were filling with people, some audibly praying, others shouting – all afraid.

"Tita, hurry! They're going to bomb Agana soon!" someone yelled.

She ran as fast as she could with the crying baby. Exhausted, she arrived at her parents' home to find a scene similar to ones she had passed in flight – people evacuating their houses, the look of fear on their faces.

"Daughter, daughter, thank Mary in heaven you are here!" Mama Pai cried. "We must go! Get in the jitney! ... Here, take Chris!"

"In a daze, Mariquita obeyed. She sat down in the back of the jitney with her two babies. People and things were being jammed around her. Soon the jitney was making its way out of the city along roads that were a confusion of people, carabao carts and other vehicles. Most of the people were walking, entire families bunched together and carrying as much as they could manage. "*La chaddek!* Hurry!" Behind them to the south, black smoke boiled into the sky. Gaining her composure, Mariquita looked about her.

"Where's Papa and the others?" she asked her mother.

"They're still at the house," Mama Pai answered. "Papa, Johnny and Frankie will join us later. There wasn't enough room for them." Hanging her head in anguish, Mama Pai began praying, "Oh, my dear God, please protect them."

"Mama, Mama, don't worry. They'll be safe," Mariquita said comforting her. And then, turning to her own worry, she prayed silently for Eddie.

Uncle Juan Aguon, Mama Pai's brother, drove the packed jitney. He had come to Agana earlier expecting to take the family to the picnic. In the jitney were Da, Pepe, Walter, Felix, Joseph, Carmen, Mama Pai, Mariquita and the two children. Uncomfortable as they were, no one complained. They left most of the city's confusion behind them and rode in silence. The older occupants were in a state of shock and the children, sensing the adult's fear, kept quiet. Upon reaching Tumon Bay, they turned off the main road onto a narrow jungle road that led to Pepe's ranch where there was a crude shelter. While the others unloaded provisions they had brought with them and set up the emergency camp, Mariquita took care of her children. After feeding Helen again, she diapered her with a piece of cloth torn from a bed sheet. Making a crib out of an empty canned-milk box, she placed Helen in it, loosely wrapped in the hospital baby blanket she had taken with her, and covered the top of the box with a small square of mosquito netting she had found in the shelter.

The older family members were deeply troubled by what had occurred but didn't talk much about it, wanting to keep their fears to themselves. When the immediate chores were finished and the family was resting, Pepe came over to Mariquita and quietly told her of the events he saw that morning. He told her that he was at work with the Pomeroy Construction crew on Cabras Island when the Japanese planes flew over, bombing the town of Sumay, the Navy Yard and landing docks at Piti, and the *Penguin* as she sailed out of the harbor. He did not know what happened to the ship as he had left immediately for Agana, but he did see the *Penguin* firing its guns at the planes. Mariquita, holding back tears, looked down at her son who was snuggled in her arms and began to sing an old Chamorro song to him about a beautiful bird in a tree.

An gumupu si paluma
Ya tumohge' gi trongkon donne'
Ya ha tågo' yu' si Nåna
Na i bunita bai hu konne'

Several hours later, Uncle Juan decided to leave for the city, hoping to bring the others to the ranch. After he left, the boys were sent to gather firewood and coconuts, and while Carmen watched the babies, Mariquita helped Da prepare the food that had been intended for the picnic, and Mama Pai and Pepe began weaving palm fronds into sleeping mats.

Juan and the others had not arrived by the time the family finished eating and Mama Pai began to worry and anxiously listen for the sound of the jitney coming up the road. She was looking over at Mariquita and her grandchildren when Walter spotted planes coming from the direction of Saipan.

"Hurry! Into the jungle!" he yelled. Mariquita grabbed Helen from her make-shift crib and looked for Chris. She saw Walter pick him up and carry him. She clutched Helen tightly to her and joined the family in their headlong scramble into the jungle. Hidden, they heard the planes drone overhead, and shortly afterwards, the sounds of bombing and gunfire in the distance.

Mariquita could no longer contain her fear and anger and cried out, "Why are you doing this? Please dear God, please make them stop! Please, please, please, make them stop."

Da made her way to the sobbing young mother and took the baby in her arms while Mama Pai held her daughter close.

"Now, now, my little girl. Do not fear," Mama Pai told her. "Let's go sit under that tree and pray."

The enemy planes, their mission completed, zoomed back over

them in the direction from which they came, and the family remained huddled in the jungle for some time. When they thought it was safe, they ventured into a clearing, the sunlight a welcome relief from the damp darkness that had sheltered them. It was then out of fear of death that Mariquita had Auntie Da baptize Helen.

The beleaguered family remained in the jungle sanctuary the remainder of that day and night. Pepe occasionally returned to the shelter to see if the others had arrived. On one of his returns, he told them that all the lights in the city were out.

Just before dawn, Papa, Frankie and Johnny arrived on foot, their shouts alerting the anxious family to their presence. Papa told them that Juan had remained in the city because the government needed all available vehicles. The trio brought with them food, clothing and bedding. Papa also reported that most of the people had left the city, and that it was almost deserted except for some military personnel. Agana suffered little damage, he reported. Only a few stores and houses had been bombed, but the planes had machine-gunned the hospital and streets. Several people were said to have been killed and some wounded.

He had also heard that most of the Navy and Marine facilities, the Cable Station, the Pan American Airways Hotel and service buildings, and the Standard Oil tanks were also bombed. Stories were circulating and one was that some of the Japanese nationals living on the island had been spying for Japan and had provided information on the location of the targets.

All of the Japanese had been rounded up and confined at the Agana jail. As for the *Penguin*, Papa had heard that it had been bombed and some crewmembers had made it ashore safely, but that was all he knew. He was unable to offer any first-hand knowledge since he and the boys had stayed in the house, securing it and getting things ready for their journey. Their only contacts were the few people who passed by. They would all have to wait and pray that Eddie was safe.

With the dawn, the planes returned and like a repeat of the

previous day, the sounds of bombing and gunfire were heard in the distance. After the planes had accomplished their mission and left, the family decided to move higher up to a cave on Auntie Rita Aguon's property where they would be safer.

Hiking through the jungle terrain to the cave was difficult. The men had to take turns cutting the way clear with machetes. Besides this, the supplies and Mariquita's two babies had to be carried, eight-year-old Carmen and seven-year-old Joseph had to be watched and sometimes assisted, and Auntie Da had to be led. The climb was long and steep, but they did not stop until they reached the ledge at the mouth of the cave. The cave was musty, with numerous cobwebs and annoying insects, but it appeared to be a safe hiding place. It was high up on the cliff facing Tumon Bay and they could see clearly if anyone was coming. It was also large enough to accommodate the whole family and their provisions, but it was dark not far inside and on their first inspection, Joseph banged his head against a rock, requiring compresses and bandaging.

The family worked hard cleaning up the portion of the cave near the entrance and burned coconut husks to smoke out the insects. In late afternoon, they prepared and ate their evening meal and remained outside until after sunset.

Mariquita slept fitfully that night, awakening often. Lying in the darkness wrapped in a blanket with her babies at her side, she could barely see the moonlit mouth of the cave and a small array of stars through her tears. She was frightened for Eddie and angry at what had happened to her island. She fell asleep again only to awaken a short time later. At the cave's entrance was the silhouette of a man. Thinking that it might be Eddie, she arose quietly and crept to him. It was Walter, her brother. Pointing, he said, "Tita, look!"

Out beyond the reef were several ghost-looking ships, and flares were lighting the sky. As they stood there, transfixed by the incredible sight, the menacing sound of gunfire came from a distance.

The sounds awakened the others. Chris, finding the comforting presence of his mother gone, began to cry, and soon Helen was crying, too. They were picked up, and soon everyone was at the mouth of the cave, their reserved box for the end of the first act of war. Silently, the entire family witnessed the invasion of their island.

They stood there in the early morning darkness for a long time. As the sun rose, they watched as sampans and other small boats left the enemy ships to disembark troops, horses, supplies and various other instruments of war on their shore. As Japanese soldiers passed below their angle of sight, they returned to the security of the cave, with horror-stricken thoughts of what was happening.

By noon, most of the landing activities had ceased and the invading forces had left the immediate area. Pepe and Johnny were sent to contact others in the surrounding jungle. When they returned, they sadly related that they had learned that the Governor had surrendered the island. They also said that everyone was ordered to go to Agana to register with the Japanese Imperial Forces. Even the children had to go. The evils of conquest had begun.

6
Prologue to Pain

TOWARD THE LATTER PART of 1941, the Navy increased the complement of the *USS Penguin*, adding three more officers and several enlisted men to the crew. About the same time, two YP boats (small patrol craft) were brought to Guam to alternate with the *Penguin* on twenty-four-hour patrols around the island.

Sunday, December 7, was the *Penguin's* turn to cruise slowly around the island on the lookout for anything unusual. Nothing was sighted and never had been on any patrol. In fact, nothing of significance had occurred since the *Saibo Maru* had floundered off Guam nearly a year before. The *Penguin* had rescued some 20 survivors but then had difficulty getting rid of them. The Governor had ordered the *Penguin* to take the Japanese to Rota, about forty miles north of Guam, but the ship had been fired upon as it came near the island and had to turn back. Permission had been requested from the Japanese authorities on Saipan to take them there, but the request had been denied. Finally, arrangements were made to rendezvous with the inter-island steamer *Saipan Maru* a few miles off Guam to off-load the human cargo.

The Japanese had been interrogated at the time of rescue. They had claimed to be fishermen, but the general consensus on the *Penguin* was that they were spies. As John Zahnen told Eddie at the time, "Their hands are not the hands of fishermen."

Guam in 1941 was vulnerable to attack and occupation by even the weakest enemy. For twenty years, the island had been demilitarized, a tiny unprotected bit of U.S. real estate in the far Pacific Ocean, just like a soldier on a battlefield without a weapon. Even after Japan's arrogant aggression in East Asia, the Congress of the United States refused to appropriate funds for the island's defense.

At 8 a.m. on Monday, the *Penguin* steamed back into Apra Harbor, its twenty-four hours of patrol duty completed. As soon as it tied up to the buoy, Eddie and the rest of the boiler room crew shut off steam to the main engines and left the place in the hands of the man who had the first in-spot watch. Eddie was off duty and anxious to go ashore. He wanted to celebrate the Feast Day with Mariquita, and planned to attend the *Penguin*'s annual beach party that afternoon before joining the Perez family at the Unpingco ranch.

As Eddie walked out onto the main deck, a station boat from the Piti Navy Yard came alongside. A messenger ran up the gangway and delivered a note to the captain, Lieutenant J. W. Haviland III. The captain read the note and shouted, "Get underway immediately!" As Eddie ran for the boiler room, the general quarters' (battle station) alarm sounded. He wondered momentarily just what was in that note, but since he was in charge of the boiler room, he had other things to think about.

The boiler room crew worked feverishly to get the steam pressure cut in again to the main engines. The voice tube bell rang and Eddie listened in amazement as the engine room chief told him that the captain had ordered the ship cut loose from the buoy and that the ship was adrift. If they did not get the ship moving and under control soon, he thought, they would end up on a reef.

"We're loose from the buoy!" Eddie shouted to his crew.

"To hell with warm-up time! Cut those boilers in at full power NOW!" In desperation, the men acted. The ship slowly picked up speed. Eddie could tell by the roll of the ship that they were nearing the rough water at the mouth of the harbor.

Suddenly gunfire was heard overhead. Eddie was sure that all of the *Penguin*'s guns were firing: the two three-inch antiaircraft deck guns and a couple of .50 caliber machine guns. The ship shook with each volley from the deck guns, even causing insulation to break loose from the overhead piping and fall down on the heads of the crew below. "This is some drill," Eddie thought, "it's almost as if we're firing at something."

He learned they were firing at something – Japanese planes! The boiler room crew talked about this unbelievable state of affairs, but none of them could make any sense of it. The firing ceased. It was quiet and remained so for some time. The ship continued to steam through the calm waters off Apra Harbor. There was no more talk. Everyone was intent on performing their duty.

The firing began again, and a bomb exploded near the ship. Holes appeared in the side of the ship on the port side of the boiler room. Fireman L.W. McKenzie was wounded and blood was running down the side of his head. It was all so unreal, obviously dangerous, yet very exciting to Eddie. No one could guess what lay ahead.

The *Penguin* began to slow down. It became quiet again, much quieter than before. Eddie decided to find out what was happening, so he climbed the ladder and opened the door into the mess hall. He walked through the mess hall to one of the doors leading out onto the main deck. He opened the door to see a wall of flames, and a tremendous noise filled his ears. A second bomb had exploded in front of him. Now frightened, and having no business being up out of the boiler room, he slammed the door and rushed down the ladder just as a third bomb exploded. The *USS Penguin* was now dead in the water.

It was quiet again, deathly quiet. In the boiler room, Eddie and the five other boiler crewmen waited, and waited. He rang the bell to the engine room, listening on the voice tube for an answer. There was no response. He continued ringing and listening. The boiler crew took wrenches and pounded on the bulkhead separating them from the engine room, but still no response.

"They're all dead out there, I guess," Eddie told his men.

"What are we going to do?" one of them asked.

"We're going to stay right here," he replied firmly. It was what Eddie had been taught. "No one left his assigned post, especially his battle station, in a war, and this must be war," he thought.

The door to the boiler room opened above them. "Is everybody out down there?" a strange voice called down.

Eddie thought it was a Japanese voice. He looked at the others, saying, "We've been boarded. We might as well go up."

The voice was not Japanese and the ship had not been boarded. It was the executive officer making his last rounds on the sinking ship. The men went topside to find everyone else heading to shore. Someone had forgotten to tell the boiler room crew!

They found enough life jackets for all of them in the storage lockers. When they were ready, they jumped over the side together. The ship was about two miles from the island, and the men kept watching the sky for the planes they feared would return to strafe them. They made it safely to shore.

The entire island was in a state of shock. In addition to the random bombings, villages and roads had been bombed. No one knew how many had been killed and wounded. The *Penguin*'s survivors headed for Agana to the Governor's Palace, the Navy headquarters that would serve as a command post. En route, they learned of the bombing of Pearl Harbor and that Robert White, Marian's fiancé, had been killed in the bombing of the *Penguin*.

Eddie thought of his family, his wife and newborn daughter at the hospital and his son. But he was first a fighting man in the service of his country, and his military duty took priority.

Although the events were altogether too real, it was like a movie, one in which he was an actor. A great drama, a world drama! One, he hoped, would surely have a happy ending.

Except for the activity around the Governor's Palace, Agana was deserted. The slow pace that had characterized the city disappeared in the dust of the refugees. At the Governor's Palace, the military personnel were being assigned to various posts. Eddie and a shipmate, Machinist Mate Verne Bairey, were sent to the Agana Power Plant to assist in keeping it in operation. McKenzie, the crewman who had been wounded, was taken to the hospital.

Eddie and Verne joined the Guamanian workers at the power plant. It had not been damaged. And when Japanese planes returned that afternoon, bombing and strafing the city, the power plant remained intact, perhaps not targeted by the enemy. As a whole, Agana sustained little damage. That night, Eddie and Verne slept in a small building next to the plant. Early the following morning, the planes returned. This time a few houses and stores were hit. From a friend of one of the Guamanian workers, Eddie learned that the Perez family, including Mariquita and the children, had fled the city and were in Tumon.

That evening, the workers decide that they, too, should leave. They told the two sailors that they had been informed by Saipanese sent to the island of a coming invasion, but Eddie and Verne dismissed it as merely a rumor. They were left alone in the plant. Since they could not operate the big coal burning boilers and generators by themselves, the fires were allowed to die out and the generators to shut down. Some Navy and Marine Corps personnel and a portion of the Guam Insular Force were about the only people left in the city. That night, Agana was in total darkness. The two men went to the building next-door and dropped off to sleep, exhausted.

Early Wednesday morning, December 10, they were awakened by gunshots.

"I'm going to run over to the plant and climb up to see what's happening," Eddie told Verne. As he dashed around the corner at the back of the plant, he ran into Japanese soldiers.

Stopped short by their unexpected and menacing presence, Eddie raised his hands in surrender. In front of him, in killing stance, were several Japanese soldiers who could have come to life from the stereotyped pictures he had seen. In full combat dress, fitted with camouflage materials on their heads and shoulders and poised with fixed bayonets, they confronted him. With his heart beating furiously, Eddie cautiously hollered to Verne, "They got me! Better come out slowly!"

Verne came out, and the soldiers dragged him roughly to Eddie's side. With their captors directing them with grunts and prods, they were marched to the front of the power plant facing the ocean. There, standing before them with contempt etched on his face, was a Japanese officer. He barked a command to the soldiers, and those nearest ripped Eddie and Verne's shirts off them. They turned them around with their backs to the officer. The last Eddie saw of the officer was his raised sword, a glint of sunlight dancing off the blade. Frightened, Eddie thought, this can't be real, but he bowed his head, resigned to a beheading. He waited for the blow.

The blow did not come. For almost an hour they stood there. Then the soldiers took them and shoved them into a truck. They wondered what had saved them, surely not the soldiers' mercy. They both believed that they were going to be killed, but instead they were to be humiliated and degraded before the Guamanian people as proof of Japanese superiority. They were taken to the Plaza. The surrounding areas were filled with thousands of troops. Eddie and Verne joined the other American and Guamanian prisoners who were sitting in the hot sun in front of the Palace. Most of them – including the Governor - were in their underwear. Some were naked. Many were wounded and some were dead or dying. Whatever the captors liked, such as watches and rings, they took. The prisoners were taught to bow in the presence of the Japanese, the importance of doing so being demonstrated when one of the prisoners refused, and, in one swift motion, was disemboweled with a bayonet.

Eddie watched as others joined their pathetic assembly. He saw beatings, kicks and blows from rifle butts. However, it was not until he learned that the American flag was hauled down and degraded and saw the Japanese flag flying that Eddie's mind accepted the horror of the day.

Eddie tried not to think. He was hungry and thirsty, and his face and shoulders were burning from the hot sun. Sometime around noon, a Japanese officer stood on a table, and through an interpreter, proclaimed the occupation of the island. He said the people were to meet the army's needs, and those who defied them or acted as spies would be shot.

The prisoners were later herded into the Insular Guard headquarters. It was "standing-room only" on Eddie's first of 1,365 nights of captivity.

7

The Island in Turmoil

THE JAPANESE INVASION FORCE, consisting of about five hundred men of a special landing unit backed up by war ships, planes and over five thousand troops, had confronted a defensive unit of about one hundred Guards of the Insular Force. Organized earlier that year, the Insular Guards and the few Americans at the Plaza de España were armed with only four machine guns and a small number of rifles, some were World War I vintage with the words "Do Not Fire - For Training Only" burned into the stock.

U.S. military personnel on the island numbered 427, of which almost two-thirds were in the administrative, hospital and communication branches. Many of those capable of fighting had been scattered on the first day of pre-invasion bombing. Of those who remained to take up defensive positions, most were in the Sumay area. The Governor, Navy Captain George J. McMillian, ordered Chief Lane, the Chief Boatswain's Mate who was in command of the Insular Guard, to post the machine guns around the Plaza, and to man them with local guardsmen. They were to keep up a "delaying fire" for at least twenty minutes, then surrender if the enemy appeared in overwhelming force.

Gunfire was heard as the first column of Japanese troops approached the city. Six sailors from the sunken *Penguin* engaged the enemy in combat but were immediately overrun, shot and bayoneted. A Guamanian civilian fired at the enemy from the window of his house; the enemy retaliated with a flamethrower, burning the house to the ground and roasting the man alive. As the troops neared the Cathedral, the Plaza defenders opened fire and drove the enemy back. The troops advanced a second time and were again driven back. A number of men had been killed and wounded.

Another column of enemy troops was approaching by way of the Leary School and a third column from behind the Plaza. Chief Lane warned the Governor, "We must surrender at once to save lives. It is no longer possible to resist." The Governor went upstairs to change into his uniform.

Commander Giles, second in command, and Chief Lane stepped out of the Palace waving a white handkerchief. They ran to an automobile parked in front and sounded the horn three times. A Japanese officer blew a whistle, and the firing ceased. A voice ordered the senior officers to come across the Plaza under a flag of truce and surrender.

As Giles and Lane started across the Plaza, five defenders, unaware that the surrender was in progress, fired on the approaching second column of enemy troops and were instantly killed. Hearing the gunfire, four men in the Governor's office ran out the back into a volley of rifle fire. Two were killed, the third severely wounded and bayoneted, and the fourth taken prisoner.

A Japanese officer met Giles and Lane and placed them under arrest as prisoners of war. They were marched the short distance to the Agana Navy Yard on the waterfront to surrender to the Japanese general who was in command of enemy forces. They were then returned to the Plaza and accompanied by the general who demanded the formal surrender of the island by the Governor.

Later that morning, the Perez family walked the three miles from Tumon to Agana. It was a walk of horror. Overturned cars and dead bodies were piled by the wayside. Prior to that time, the only dead bodies the family had seen were those properly prepared for burial. It was an unbelievable scene. Foreign troops in combat uniform, helmeted and wearing split-toed rubber-soled shoes were every-where, shouting words the family did not understand.

Even harder for them to believe was the sight that faced them in Agana. It had been completely overrun by Japanese troops, horses and equipment; government buildings, schools, the hospital, some shops and homes, and even their beloved Cathedral were now occupied by the foreigners; and looting and destruction of property was going on everywhere.

The family was ordered to the schoolyard of the Leary School where hundreds of Guamanians were already in line to obtain iden-tification tags. The line moved slowly and they had to endure long, miserable hours waiting their turn in the hot sun. While in line, they heard shocking stories of Japanese atrocities, witnessed some people being maltreated, and saw that prisoners were herded in front of the Palace.

When they finally reached the registration table of Japanese officials, who were using local Japanese nationals and Saipanese as interpreters, Papa was arrested and taken prisoner. He, along with others in the Insular Force, Guamanian members of the Police Force and the regular Navy, were interned in the Insular Guard headquarters.

As Papa was led away, Mama Pai cried out, "Please do not take my husband! I beg of you!" Before she had a chance to say anything else, a solider stepped forward and slapped her, threatening her with words she could not comprehend. She reeled from the blow, but managed to contain her emotions as her frightened children sought to comfort her. A local Japanese woman seeing the incident came running to her side.

"Mrs. Perez, please. You must show respect and they will not do you harm. You must not question their authority. Bow to them. Bow at the waist. The whole family must bow."

Fearful for the safety of her family, Mama Pai bowed, and the children followed her example. As soon as their registration was complete, they cautiously moved away. When they had gone a short distance, Mariquita, who had silently borne her worry over Eddie, asked the family to take the children safely home so she could find out his whereabouts. Frankie was told to accompany her and for them to be exceedingly careful.

Having heard that some men from the *Penguin* had been killed near the Pigo Cemetery south of the city, Mariquita and Frankie headed in that direction. On the way, they ran into Delia and her family. With tears in their eyes, Mariquita and Delia embraced one another.

"I've been so worried about you, Tita, with the hospital and all. Where ..."

"I know, I know," Mariquita interrupted, "but we are safe now. I am trying to find Eddie. Have you heard anything about him?"

"Tita, Eddie is one of the prisoners in the Plaza!"

"Oh, my dear God, I must go!" Mariquita said turning to leave.

"Wait! Tita, be careful!" Delia called out as she watched her friend hurrying away with Frankie.

Moving through the crowds of people and soldiers, bowing whenever they thought it might be necessary, Mariquita and Frankie made their way to an area near the bandstand, not far from the prisoners in front of the Palace. Sitting among the group of prisoners was Eddie, half naked, his head bowed. She stood staring at him, on the verge of tears, hoping that he would see her. But he did not look up. After some time, the prisoners were rounded up and marched to the Insular Guard headquarters. As Mariquita watched him leave, she said a few prayers in silence. Crying, she took hold of Frankie's hand. "Let's go, Frankie. We'll try to come back later."

The room where the prisoners were confined was crowded, and as more and more prisoners were shoved into it, it became worse. Soon there was barely enough room to move around. Eddie had caught a glance of Papa in the far corner when he had first come in and he slowly, with difficulty, made his way to him. "Papa, I'm so sorry," he said to the older grieving man as he hugged him. Fearful, he asked about Mariquita and the family. After Papa told him that they were all well, he felt a great sense of relief. Looking around, he saw many Guamanians he knew, and across the room, Marian's father.

For two days the prisoners remained there. They were given only scraps of food to eat. They were allowed very little water and had infrequent toilet privileges. This treatment was the beginning of a softening-up process to make the prisoners submissive, and it was only a hint of the cruel imprisonment many were to endure.

On Friday, the Americans were moved to Dorn Hall. Although there was more room, the conditions of imprisonment did not improve. The prisoners continued to subsist on meager rations, the food prepared by Navy cooks in the Industrial School kitchen. Meals were served only twice a day, consisting of a small piece of potato, a slice of luncheon meat and weak coffee. The following Monday they were transferred to the Cathedral, and the Guamanian prisoners replaced them in Dorn Hall.

The prisoners in the Cathedral organized themselves into groups to bring about order. This proved particularly helpful in distributing the meals, which were delivered in bulk to the Cathedral morning and evening. As for their clothing, the men shared what they had between them, but there still was not enough for each man to be fully dressed.

Nearly every day they were forced to march around the Plaza grounds. They were made to run, to stand in the hot sun, to bow, to sit, to stand ... over and over again. They slept at night on the bare wooden floor or on the church benches. The few toilet facilities were not enough, but they had to do. When they talked, they spoke quietly. They all thought that soon they would be rescued. This hope persisted despite claims by the Japanese that the U.S. fleet had been destroyed at Pearl Harbor. They did not believe the Japanese even when they were shown photographs of the destruction.

Aside from the conditions of imprisonment, their captors constantly ridiculed them. In time, Eddie felt humiliated, his pride and spirit crushed. He was ashamed that he had surrendered. He wondered if staying alive was worth it. And if he lived through this adversity, would he have the feeling that he had won over them? And should he survive, would there be some reason he was saved? For the first time, he wished his mind was not so active that it pondered such questions. He prayed and drew on his religion. Had not Jesus set an example by suffering on the cross? He began to find comfort in his faith, but Eddie's hardest tests were still to come.

The Guamanian people stood fast in their devotion to America. They bowed their bodies but not their hearts to the Japanese conquerors. They risked their lives by going to the Cathedral with gifts of food, clothing, cigarettes, anything they could manage that might ease the pain of those inside. At first, they were turned away. A few who threw their gifts over the fence surrounding the Cathedral were caught and soundly beaten.

But the Guamanians continued to go to the Cathedral daily. After a while, the Japanese, not wanting to further antagonize them, as they were needed to work on airfields, fortifications, and in food production, began accepting the offerings. After a thorough inspection, some were given to the prisoners.

Mariquita and her family regularly brought things for Papa at Dorn Hall and for Eddie at the Cathedral. Sometimes they brought enough food to be shared with others who were less fortunate, as did Mrs. Johnston and other families and friends of the prisoners. There were times, however, when the Japanese without any explanation returned the packages. But they kept going.

The few times Mariquita was able to see Eddie, she saw that he was embarrassed and downtrodden. And seeing her, he would smile, but she could tell that his smile was not real.

The only thing she could hope for was that by seeing her occasionally he would know that she was all right, and perhaps he would be less troubled.

One afternoon during the second week of imprisonment, all the Guamanian and American prisoners were marched up Tutuhan Hill.

On a spot not far from Mariquita and Eddie's special place, they were made to watch a review of the Japanese army and witness a demonstration of its firepower. They saw a general on horseback inspect the different units, which had been reduced to about three thousand men. Near the prisoners, sitting in cars as guests of honor, were about a hundred Japanese geishas and Korean "chosen," all dressed in colorful kimonos. After the inspection, machine guns opened fire on the reef fronting Agana, and then artillery pieces shelled a small island in the lagoon off Dungca's Beach. The afternoon performance ended with the shelling of a floating barge, one that was flying an American flag.

Following the spectacle, the prisoners were returned to the Plaza for a speech by a Japanese officer who told them, through an interpreter, that their lives would be spared if they were "good prisoners," otherwise, they could expect the worse. They were then taken back to their places of confinement.

The American prisoners believed that their lives would be spared, but at what cost? Many were becoming critical of their government's abandonment of them as if they were nothing more than sacrificial lambs. All cursed the Japanese, but they were afraid to organize any form of resistance, not only because of the overwhelming number of enemy troops, but also because of probable retribution against the island people.

Compounding their situation was that they were all rapidly losing weight and feeling the effects of it. But of all their difficulties, they suffered more from their loss of freedom.

There were many rumors about what was going to happen. Although they all suspected that they would not remain long in the Cathedral, few believed that they would be shipped to Japan. To confuse their thinking even more, the Spanish bishop, his secretary, and the eleven priests were now interred with them. Just before Christmas, Mariquita, along with the other wives of the prisoners, signed a petition asking the commanding general to release their husbands on Christmas Day so they could spend the holiday with their families. The request was denied. And, for the first time in over 250 years, midnight mass was not celebrated in the Cathedral.

On the afternoon of January 2, 1942, however, Eddie and the other American prisoners who had families were given permission to join them in the Plaza. He saw Mariquita as soon as he was escorted from the Cathedral. She was standing there so pretty, he thought, with Helen in her arms and Chris beside her, holding onto her skirt. Tears filled his eyes, but he brushed them away. He wanted to run to them, but caution held him back. In an unusual act of kindness, the soldiers moved away as the young couple met each other and embraced. Some time passed in tender silence before Eddie could speak.

"Tippy, you look beautiful. How much I've prayed to see you and for this to end. Here, let me see our baby. So, you named her Helen? Hi Helen, this is your daddy. How's my little girl? And my son, how's daddy's boy? Daddy loves you. Come Tippy, let's go sit over there." As soon as they sat down, he asked her softly, "Are you okay?"

"You don't need to worry about us, my darling," she said. "We're fine. It is you we must worry about. Is it so bad?"

He nodded. "It is, but we still have hope it will end soon. It's now all in God's hands. Tippy, how is the family?"

Sitting on the Plaza lawn, aware of the other family groups and the watching soldiers but not caring of their presence, Mariquita and Eddie exchanged words of reassurance, confidence and love. But Eddie did not tell Mariquita how he really felt about his imprisonment, wanting to spare her any undue worry. And when Mariquita asked Chris to say "Daddy" to make Eddie happy, he felt a pang of hurt. But Mariquita never knew his troubled feelings, as Eddie was mastering the art of concealing them.

After three weeks of forced separation, the time they had together was far too brief. But it was enough time for Mariquita and Eddie to record a mental picture they would cherish forever – the last picture of all of them together. When Eddie left, he took with him her last words, "My darling Eddie, you must not worry about us. Only take care of yourself. We will be fine and waiting for you. God bless you, my husband." On January 8, Eddie and some of the other prisoners received small packages brought by family members. In his were some clothing, toilet articles, and he and Mariquita's Bible. The arrival of the packages created many rumors. There were even more whisperings when the Governor and the prisoners who had been interred in the hospital arrived at the Cathedral the following day.

On January 10, they were awakened at 4:30 a.m. with instructions to be ready to leave by 6:30. At the appointed hour, trucks were brought to the front of the church. The bishop, priests, Navy nurses and civilians were put into some of them and the others were loaded with the baggage. The military personnel were then lined up in a column of four according to rank, with Governor McMillian, Commander W. T. Lineberry, Commander Cecha and Lieutenant Colonel MacNulty forming the front rank.

Having learned of the evacuation, hundreds of Guamanians filled the Plaza. They cried and waved when the prisoners marched by in their mismatched clothing. The Americans showed no emotion, their feelings hidden under a mantle of pride. Mariquita was there and Eddie saw her. He saw her again as she passed by the marchers in a native-owned truck. They marched five miles to the Piti Navy Yard. He saw her for the last time standing near the entrance to the Navy Yard gate. She was waving. That sweet image of her, so beautiful and full of love, was captured in his mind forever.

8
Occupation

MARIQUITA, DRESSED IN THE dark blue dress that was Eddie's favorite, stood apart from the small group of Guamanians who had boldly gathered to bid farewell to the departing Americans at the entrance to the Piti Navy Yard. She and Pepe had risked their lives to get there. All of the motor vehicles had been confiscated by the Japanese, but for the most part, were still scattered about the city and unguarded. Mariquita located a truck formerly owned by a neighbor and asked him for his spare key. After warning her about the danger involved, he gave her the key and she and Pepe stole the truck and drove to Piti.

Watching the column of weary men approaching, Mariquita could not hold back her tears. She tried to dry them, but by the time Eddie marched by, her face was wet again. For one brief moment their eyes met. She bravely held her head high, waved and sent him her love. Then she made the sign of the cross.

After the Americans had disappeared from view, Pepe gently led Mariquita back to the truck where she changed into the blouse and slacks she had brought with her. They had decided that if they made it to Piti, they would not push their luck by trying to drive back. Sadly, they walked the long road to Agana, Mariquita imagining that she was retracing Eddie footsteps.

In the road in front of the family home, Mama Pai met her grief-stricken daughter. She took Mariquita in her waiting arms, saying, "Tita, the only thing you can do now for Eddie is pray for him. I understand your sorrow, my daughter, but you must live for the day he returns and take care of yourself and your children. God will be with him."

"But Mama, I don't want to live. My life went with Eddie," Mariquita sobbed.

"Now, now ... quiet," Mama Pai said, as she brushed the hair off her daughter's face. "Look at me." Then, holding her at arm's length, she looked into her eyes and said sternly, "I do not want you to say that ever again. Your life is here with your children. And Mama needs you."

Mama Pai was a kind and sensitive woman, but when the need arose, she became the strength of her family. Holding Mariquita, she led her to the outside kitchen in back of the house and comforted her. Sometime later, Mariquita went to her room to rest.

She tried to sleep, but could not. As if watching a movie, she saw her life with Eddie unwind before her eyes. When the final reel ended, she was once again in tears. She thought of how much she hated the Japanese barbarians who had disrupted their happy life and then had taken her husband away from her. What had Eddie and his fellow prisoners done to them? It was one thing to imprison them, but why the move to Japan, and why had they been so cruel to the already beaten Americans while they were imprisoned? And, why were they so cruel to her people?

This was the first time Mariquita knew the meaning of hate, and the hatred she felt, frightened her. She turned to God for understanding and direction. As if she heard a voice, she remembered the saying, "Love your enemies, bless them that curse you, do good to them that hate you, and pray for them that despitefully use you, and persecute you." Was God speaking to her, or did it come to mind from reading the Bible with Eddie? Mariquita wasn't sure.

Her movements for the next several weeks were limited to those of necessity. The family picked up her share of work and responsibilities, giving her time to come to terms with the awful reality of the present.

As she came to grips with her grief, her physical strength increased. She became determined to survive this ordeal.

Mariquita and her children remained at the family home. Even if she had wanted to, she could not have gone back to her own house. At first Japanese troops had ransacked it, taking all the food supplies, emptying the drawers and cabinets, and destroying Eddie's uniforms and other things American, including a framed picture of Eddie's parents, whom she had hoped to meet that very year. They had also ripped some of the siding off the house for firewood, and litter was scattered everywhere. Later, it was fixed up and occupied by some Japanese military personnel.

Only once had Mariquita gone there, and that was soon after the surrender when everything was intact. With Johnny's help, she had been able to retrieve some things, including the Bible she had given to Eddie. She was planning on returning to get more things, but when Johnny told her about the destruction, she felt violated and never wanted to go back.

Papa and the other Guamanian prisoners were forced to work at various sites loading and unloading ships and performing other hard labor. Shortly after the Americans left, they were split up and sent to several smaller camps. When the Japanese army departed, leaving only a small garrison of around four hundred navy men and civilian officials, some of the prisoners were released. Papa was one of them, but he returned home a beaten man. The things he had endured during his confinement permanently scarred him.

He turned to the land to ease his mind, and began farming in order to raise food for the family. At first, he would rise early in the morning and walk to the ranch in Chalan Pago, returning to the city before sundown. Sometimes he would hitch up the carabao to the cart and haul his farm products to the city. But later, he remained at the ranch, going to the city only on weekends. Finally, he absolutely refused to go to the city and stayed at the ranch most of the time.

At the beginning of the occupation, it was impractical for the entire family to move to the ranch, as it would be sometime before the amount of food would make them somewhat self-sufficient. It was better for them to remain in the city and together try to eke out a living. Their main concern was food. Rationing of food and clothing had begun soon after the surrender, but the food supplies were quickly exhausted and the only remaining store with any food was the Japanese-owned *Kohatsu*.

The currency in use was now the Japanese yen. Although they were given several days to exchange their U.S. dollars, the Guamanians were confident that the Americans would soon liberate them, and very little money was exchanged. After the food supplies vanished, it made no difference anyhow.

As time went by, the family's food supply became scarce and they had to barter to survive. They depended primarily upon fishing and the making of salt from boiling seawater, which they often traded for food. The latter required a lot of firewood, and the children were kept busy bringing in wood from the outskirts of Agana. They looked mostly for the branches of the *gågu* tree, whose wood burned more slowly.

During the Japanese Naval rule from March 1942 to March 1944, Guamanians lived in fear and hardship, but conditions were relatively better than they had been during the first three months following the invasion, primarily because there were fewer troops. The propaganda message of the Japanese was that they planned to rule the island for one thousand years as part of the "Greater East Asia Co-Prosperity Sphere" – a coalition of self-sufficient Asian nations led by Japan without Western influence.

Efforts were made to persuade the Guamanian people to cooperate, but the cooperation would never be realized. Besides their unwavering loyalty to America, the Guamanians had seen enough during the first three months of the occupation to turn them solidly against Japan.

Those three months were so horrible to the peace-loving, gentle people of Guam that in Agana, where once lived half of the island's population of 22,000, less than two hundred families remained, and the majority of them were living on the outskirts. During those first three months, there were countless incidents of brutality, and on a small island where very little could be kept secret, everyone knew about them. Additionally, most horrifying to the people, were the atrocious acts committed in public.

One day, not long after Eddie and Papa were imprisoned, Johnny came home with an eyewitness account of the execution by a firing squad of Alfred L.G. Flores and Francisco B. Won Pat. Johnny had been on his way home when he was forced into a truck and taken to the Pigo Cemetery. Along with others who had been brought there, including women and children, he was made to watch the execution. Flores had been accused of smuggling a note in a plate of rice to his American civilian co-worker who was interned in the Cathedral; Won Pat was charged with stealing goods from the Pomeroy Company warehouse in Sumay. Both young men had been severely tortured before their executions.

Under the naval control, the Guamanians fared somewhat better, but the brutalities and atrocities continued, most of them committed by the Japanese police and their interpreters. The Guamanians who suffered the worst torture were those accused of helping the few American servicemen who had not been captured and were thought to be in hiding.

The "Japanization" of Guam peaked during the summer of 1942. The island and all of the

Guam under Japanese control. (M.A.R.C. Photo Collection)

villages had been given Japanese names and schools were re-opened to teach Japanese language and traditions. All American books were burned. Young children were required to attend classes each morning, but instead of pledging allegiance to the American flag, they now bowed to the emperor of Japan. If they were late for school, they were slapped or struck with sticks. People between the ages of thirteen and sixty had to attend evening classes twice a week. Gradually, as more people began living in semi-seclusion in rural areas and others found excuses for not attending, few adults were left in the education program.

The Gaiety Theater was re-opened to show Japanese films. Cintero Okada, who had worked for Mr. Johnston for several years and who was one of several of Japanese descent who remained loyal to America, operated the projector. Prior to the invasion, he had helped destroy military property to keep it from falling into enemy hands. "I'm in a hell of a spot," he told Mr. Johnston when he was allowed to visit him in the Cathedral after the surrender, "the Japanese do not trust me because I worked for the Americans, and the Guamanians do not trust me because I am Japanese."

One of the films shown was of the American prisoners in Japan. It had been widely publicized, and Mariquita went to see it. She saw Eddie in the film, which had been taken at a prison camp in Japan. It was the only movie she had seen since the occupation and would be the last film she would ever see. But just knowing that Eddie was alive helped fuel the fire within her and gave her strength. She worked hard, all the while protectively sheltering Chris and Helen from the harsh realities of the occupation. They were never to know hunger or the extent of her unhappiness. The Perez family became a loving, working, survival unit, and other Guamanian families matched this unity. Together they epitomized the noble character of their Chamorro heritage.

Mariquita spent most of her time making salt and bartering. When clothing material became scarce, she began trading her cloth ing for food. And since most of the people had left the city, she was compelled to walk great distances to trade, often accompanied by one of her brothers, a girl friend or a neighbor. Soon, she lost all the weight she had gained during her pregnancy.

Despite the hardships, Mariquita rarely complained, and maintaining her pride, she always appeared neat and well dressed, almost as if she was denying the harsh reality of life around her. To many, she was like a pretty flower in an otherwise dreary landscape. She seldom went into the center of the city because of the Japanese soldiers. She disliked having to bow to everything Japanese – every person, sentry box, office, and even living quarters that she passed. On one of the few occasions she did go to Agana, she saw Marian.

Marian had been given the choice of laboring at a worksite or continuing the operation of her family's beauty shop. Deciding to run the shop, her customers were almost exclusively the geisha and Korean girls who paid her a few yen each. Very few Guamanian girls came to the shop. When they did, it was after regular shop hours, and Marian did their hair for ranch produce or whatever the girls could spare.

Mariquita could not afford such a personal luxury, and she was too proud to accept when her friend offered to do her hair for nothing. It hurt Marian to see how much Mariquita had changed. She seemed to be well, but she was thin and her eyes revealed deep hurt and sadness. When Marian tried to talk to her about it, she replied, "Oh, I'm just like everyone else, having a rough time, but getting along."

Concerned, Marian pressed her with more questions, only to have Mariquita respond abruptly, "I just don't want to talk about it!" Their conversation turned to a lighter vein, but when Mariquita left, Marian burst into tears.

As times became harder and the difficulties increased, Chris and Helen became even more precious to their mother. Seeing them at the end of a tiring day of working and bartering was her reward, and she attended lovingly to their every need.

"One day," she told Mama Pai," Helen will grow up to become a beautiful dancer." She had already decided that Chris should become a priest. Without knowing it, Mariquita herself was nearing her God.

The devotion of the Guamanian people to the church and its teachings helped sustain them. Only three of God's shepherds were left on the island: two Catholic priests, Father Jesus Baza Duenas and Father Oscar Lujan Calvo, and one Baptist minister, the Reverend Joaquin Flores Sablan. They ministered to their flock when they could, usually in secluded locations. But for the most part, individual families held religious observances during the years of the occupation.

As the Perez family's goods diminished, all of those who were old enough worked for the family's survival. Often, however, Johnny and Frankie were assigned to help fill the daily work quota imposed by the Japanese, usually being sent to work in the manganese mines. For this they received a few yen a month and an occasional ration coupon for a cup of raw rice. Later, they would not receive even these meager tokens, and would have to share the little food they brought with them with their Japanese guards.

Frequently they were abused, sometimes for not bringing enough food, or merely for the pleasure of their overseers. When they were not filling work quotas, they helped the women make salt, bartered, helped Walter fish and went to the ranch and helped Papa tend to the taro, yams, corn and other food crops. They also gathered coconuts and wild fruit from the jungle and tended the livestock. The city boys learned the rural arts quickly and well.

By the end of the first year of Japanese naval rule, the family was getting by, having adjusted to the rigors of life under the Japanese flag. And because of their courage and industry, they were on their way to achieving a state of self-sufficiency.

Mariquita, growing accustomed to her new way of life, determinedly lived one day at a time. She prayed for Eddie daily and continued her unstinting care of the children. Toward the end of the month of March in 1943, she heard that brief letters to the American prisoners of war in Japan would be accepted by their families and forwarded to them. She hurriedly wrote her letter to Eddie.

Akashi, Omiya Yima
March 26, 1943

My Dearest Ed,

I am taking this opportunity to write to you and tell you that we are all well and hope that you are the same.

The children are growing very fast, especially your girl Helen Evelyn. She is already walking and can say a few words like pretty flowers, daddy, ma, pig, and cake. She is an image of you except that she takes after my nose (more perfect of course). Chris makes a good errand boy and takes care of his sister while I am at work. We all miss you, but what can we do? Only pray for peace to come soon so that we can see each other again.

Please write when you have a chance. We all want to hear from you.

I love you always.

Love and kisses,
Your wife and children
TIPPY

9
Uneasy Peace

Eddie received only one letter from Mariquita while he was a prisoner of war in Japan. For a long time, he stood outside his barracks wanting to be alone with his thoughts of her. He read the letter over and over, thinking how far away she was, yet so close in his memory.

He looked at the familiar handwriting on the envelope, and the unfamiliar Japanese name for Agana and Guam (Akashi, the red city, and Omiya Jima, the great shrine island, were the names given by the Japanese government upon capture of the island). He wondered why the letter had been typed. Was she being careful so there would be no question that the letter would pass the censors, or was it a typed copy of her original letter? And why had she chosen to address him as Ed when he had always been Eddie to her? The seriousness of the tone disturbed him, but the letter did ease his concern for her and the children. He would always treasure this letter, as it would be his last from her. He kept it throughout and after the war.

Since leaving Guam on the passenger liner *Argentina Maru* and surviving the five-day nightmare voyage in steerage to the port of Takamatsu on the island of Shikoku, Eddie had been in several prison camps beginning at Zentsuji and now was confined at Camp Hirohata in Osaka on the main island of Honshu.

He had suffered greatly. He slaved at worksites, lived with continual hunger, saw his weight drop from 145 to 100 pounds and

Eddie as a Prisoner of War in Japan.
(Perez Howard Photo Collection)

endured physical and mental abuse from his captors. He was infested with lice, harbored diseases and suffered from the elements. As one general told the prisoners, "It is the aim of Japan to give its prisoners as much pain as humanity will allow," and Eddie was testimony to the truth of this statement. He was the sad travesty of a once strong, healthy and happy young man.

As the difficulty of survival became more severe, Eddie withdrew into himself, and his friends from Guam who were with him became mere shadows of a past life. God became Eddie's companion. Often Eddie would talk with him, and although he tried to get God to answer, God never spoke, at least not out loud.

Eddie was the only person in the camp with a Bible and because of this, he was singled out to witness the cremation of fellow prisoners who died. He would pray for them as their bodies were reduced to ashes. He often asked, "Why me Lord?" but he continued in his religious role without regret and would also hold prayer services. During this time, he memorized over 250 Bible verses that he would recite to himself on the marches to and from the steel mill where he was assigned to work.

It was March 1944 and a year had passed since Mariquita had written her letter to Eddie and over two years since she had last seen him on that unhappy day of his departure. Although she did not know if he was still alive, in her heart she felt he was, and as she sat on the riverbank in the jungle, where she had taken Chris and Helen to bathe and wash clothes, she prayed for him.

The whole family was now living in Chalan Pago after the air raid on Orote Point by American planes the month before forced their evacuation from the city. The Japanese, aware of the Guamanians' unfaltering loyalty to the Americans, wanted them away from their encampments except during working hours. The Perez family's home in Agana was used as a Japanese outpost.

Having to vacate their Agana home worried the family somewhat, but over the past year, most of the members had permanently moved to the ranch before being taken over by the Japanese.

Prior to the evacuation, Mariquita had gone to the city several times alone as the older boys were now forced to work more often. The Japanese authorities had ordered larger daily worker quotas be filled by each village and the districts of Agana. At times, on these trips, Mariquita would be accompanied by others, who were also going to the city. On several occasions she took Helen with her, even though the three-mile walk on the coral road with several steep hills was a difficult undertaking. She did this in order to be able to spend more time with her baby, and also to identify herself as a young mother. She hoped this would afford her some protection from any soldiers she might encounter.

Walter had seen his sister late one afternoon pushing Helen in her stroller with a sack strapped to her back toward Chalan Pago as he rode past in the Japanese truck which was transporting him and other workers from the Tiyan air strip where they had worked that day. It pained him to see her struggling with the stroller and he thought of this driving spirit of hers which had helped the family to survive the more than two years of Japanese occupation. And how beautiful she was! Despite the hardships, she always managed to look neat and pretty, and she was always ready with a smile. How much he loved her! As soon as he was let off, he ran back toward the city to help her. On reaching her side, he said, "Tita, you shouldn't be doing this alone!"

"I'm not," she laughed, looking down at her daughter who was asleep, "Helen is with me."

"You know what I mean, Tita," Walter said, taking over the chore of pushing the stroller. "It is not wise for you to go into the city without one of us."

"And how are we going to get all the things we need without

someone going into the city? With most of you working, I'm the only one who is free to go. Papa has to do the farming."

"I just don't like it."

"My dear brother, don't let it worry you so. I don't mind and it gives me a chance to see a few of my friends. Do you know how hard it is to get kerosene now?"

Walter hadn't pursued his objections. Although he did not like it, he understood the situation, and he couldn't have changed her mind anyway. If there was one thing that Mariquita was, she was stubborn. Such a beautiful, small and good sister he had, but also so strong and stubborn.

Since the recent bombings, however, Mariquita had not gone into the city as often or alone, as more Japanese soldiers began arriving on the island. She now worked on the ranch making do with what the family raised or could easily acquire. One day, she decided to spend some time away from the ranch and took her children and Carmen to the river to wash a few clothes. When she finished washing the clothes, she spread them on bushes to dry in the hot sun. Then she stretched out on a blanket under the shade of a large avocado tree that was just beginning to show signs of bearing fruit. A faint breeze passed through the stand of bamboo trees nearby, causing the leaves to shimmer. In the taller trees with their associated plants and vines, birds were flitting from branch to branch making their presence known. Chris was down at the water's edge with Carmen and Helen was beside her mother, playing with the doll Mariquita had made for her. She looked down at her daughter. The Japanese vaccinations on her arm were healing. "Why had they given four?" she wondered. "It will be the one flaw on my perfect baby, a bad reminder when Eddie and the Americans return. All of us will have these scars to remind us. And Chris, has he felt my fear? He seldom strays from me when I am home. He keeps looking back now, making sure I am not leaving without him. How quickly he is growing. He will be four in September. We'll leave soon. The clothes are almost dry."

The slow-moving stream that flowed through Ordot-Chalan Pago on its way to the ocean had become Mariquita's favorite place, replacing the one she so fondly remembered on Tutuhan Hill. It seemed far away from everything, and although it was some distance from the ranch, the jungle path made it easily accessible. Often there were other women nearby doing their wash, but this day was special because the river was theirs alone.

She thought about how relatively pleasant the past few weeks had been for the family. The older boys still had to put up with mistreatment by the Japanese at their worksites, but after their day of labor, they were able to return home. Her sister Carmen helped her with the children. And her youngest brother, Joseph, was so amusing and helpful around the ranch. The poor boy was so embarrassed when he fell off Uncle Jesus and Auntie Maria Taijeron's cow. And Felix was so happy to be home again after having to stay at the special Japanese school. That was one good thing about the recent American bombing, the schools were closed and he was able to return home.

Aside from Papa, living solely on the ranch was a new experience for most of the family members. At first, they took to farm life reluctantly, but now they were reaping the rewards of working and living on the land. Surrounding their ranch were other family ranches mostly owned by their relatives. They took comfort in this and being away from Agana and the Japanese. Although there were a few in the area, they did not have much contact with them.

At first it had been advantageous for the Perez family to live in Agana. Although most of the people had moved out, it was important as a trading center and a place to obtain information. But as time passed, the Japanese became more domineering, and when the war was not going in their favor, they became oppressive. The Perez family grew fearful and left.

During that time, Joseph had been slapped and struck with a stick by his teacher a number of times for "misbehaving." After the latest incident, he ran out of the school building and threw rocks at the windows. This had brought Japanese soldiers to the house to reprimand Mama Pai. There were other incidents involving the children that weighed heavily on Mama Pai's mind. The worst was when Johnny was taken to the police station and beaten for being out after curfew. They kicked, whipped and beat him. He later explained to Mama Pai that one of the men who took him and his friends to the police station was jealous because he liked one of the girls with them. When Johnny took off his shirt and Mama Pai saw the extent of his beating, she nearly collapsed. A couple of the men who had beat him were interpreters from Saipan and Rota. Being a headstrong young man, Johnny set about to get even. Finding out the whereabouts of the men, he gained his revenge in the dark of the night and gave them both a sound beating.

Many of the Chamorro Saipanese and Rotanese who came to the island to work for the Japanese were helpful and sympathetic to their Guamanian brothers and sisters. Others delighted in their authoritative role and they would be long remembered for their evil deeds.

With Chris now sitting watchfully beside her, Mariquita was almost asleep when Felix called in the distance. When he arrived, he helped her gather up the clothes and soon the four of them were headed home. The jungle trail they walked led to the main road that traversed the central part of the island from Agana to Pago Bay. Upon crossing the road and reaching the entrance to the ranch, several dogs met up with and accompanied them to the house.

When they arrived, Auntie Da had already started the wood fire in the open kitchen attached to the house and was preparing to cook the evening meal. Papa was feeding the pigs softened breadfruit and taro, and Mama Pai, who had faith in the powers of herbal medicine, was sitting on the front steps applying herbal leaves to a cut on Joseph's knee.

The ranch house was small, not having been built as a family home. It stood on a slope on posts, three feet high on one end to six feet high on the other, in a large clearing dominated by a huge mango tree, and surrounded by tall fruit trees and the dense jungle. The roof of the wooden house was made of tin and ladder-like steps led to its entrance. At the edge of the fringing jungle were a small outhouse, some animal pens and vegetable gardens.

Calling Carmen to care for the children, Mariquita took the laundered clothing from Felix, talked briefly with her mother, and then entered the house. "Silly," the little white dog that rarely barked yet became ferociously protective if anyone other than family came around the house, failed to move and she almost stepped on him,

There were two large rooms containing all the family's belongings, and several pieces of furniture, but no beds. In order to save space, the family now slept on woven mats, and these were rolled up and put up out of the way during the day.

Mariquita had her own section at the rear of the house for her and her children. Treasured mementos, including photographs, she kept carefully hidden in a small wooden trunk Papa had made for her when she was a little girl. Well known for his carpentry skills, Papa even made slippers with wooden soles and leather tops.

From within the house, Mariquita could hear the laughter of her children. She placed the laundry on a table near one of the open windows and as she folded the clothing, she also watched her children play.

"One day we will all go to America and stay with Mama and Papa Howard on their farm in Indiana," she thought. "Eddie told me he would buy me a fur coat to wear in the winter when it snowed. If it is as cold as he told me, I will need one."

Mariquita's hopes had been lifted by the air strike on Orote Point and she often thought about Eddie's return and their little family going to America. She knew in her heart he was still alive and she would wait for him.

The older boys arrived around 6 o'clock. They talked about the recent air raid alarms and how hard it was becoming as they tried to please their Japanese bosses. It was getting so bad at the worksites that they often showed bruises where they had been hit. Besides their own, they also told stories of worse offenses, and of other atrocities that they had heard about.

The evening passed quickly. After dinner, a smudge fire using coconut husks was started under the house to ward off mosquitoes and the boys bathed using water from the rain barrels and homemade soap. They were careful in using the water because it had not rained for some time, and when the barrels reached a certain low level, they would have to refill them by going to the water pump in Ordot. When everyone was ready for bed, the family members said their prayers, extinguished the coconut oil lamps and retired early.

The following morning, shortly after the boys left for the main road where they were picked up and transported to their worksites, Mariquita heard the dogs barking up the hill. Fearful that Japanese soldiers were coming to the house, she cautioned everyone to go inside. Papa, who was already at work gardening, was also alerted by the barking dogs and was soon at Mariquita's side.

They heard a few muffled shouts and abruptly the barking ceased. Frankie came into view with the area's *sancho*, a Guamanian appointed to serve as a minor official and messenger for the Japanese authorities.

Humbly, the *sancho* informed Papa that the Japanese had ordered higher weekly quotas of vegetables, eggs and other farm products and would need more from him to help fill the quotas. He also said that since all able-bodied Guamanian males had been ordered to work on defense projects, Papa would have to go, and Joseph would have to go to the agricultural camp in Tai with Frankie, who was already assigned there.

Alarmed that ten-year-old Joseph would have to work for the Japanese and be subjected to their mistreatment, Mariquita pleaded to take his place. The *sancho*, whose orders were only to have a certain number of people report for work at Tai, accepted the exchange.

Mariquita was afraid, but she was sure that she could fare better than her little brother. She knew of the conditions to which she would have to adjust, having been told by her brothers and others who had been to various labor sites. Up to this time, Mariquita had been fortunate in that she had not had to fill one of the worker quotas. A close friend and neighbor in Agana, Maria Cruz Perez, a sweet and lovely Chamorro girl with whom Mariquita had walked many miles on bartering trips, had been doing fieldwork for some time. When Mariquita had last seen her, she hardly recognized her and had felt sorry for her. Now she was going to join her.

Mama Pai would now be worrying about the safety of her husband and oldest daughter as well as her older boys.

10
Impending Doom

Together with the returning Japanese Army had come the *Kaikontai*, an agricultural unit whose job was to feed the military. In their desperation to meet their objectives, they were merciless. For many Guamanians, this was the beginning of an ordeal that would ultimately change their lives, and for some, it would be the beginning of their end.

As more Japanese troops arrived in anticipation of an American attack, more food was needed and soon everyone considered old enough was forced to work. Only those too young, too old or escaping detection were saved from this misery.

By June 1944, there were some 19,000 Japanese soldiers, many Koreans and approximately 24,000 Guamanians on the island. Besides working on defense projects, such as leveling airfields with their bare hands, the Guamanians were forced to feed everyone, and they were the last to be considered.

With almost everyone working on fortifications and food production for the Japanese, very few Guamanians were left to do subsistence farming on their ranches, and what was produced, and the livestock they had, were often taken by foraging troops. Many went hungry.

During this time, everyone suffered, but the ones most affected were those subjected daily to the injustice of forced labor under the scrutiny of the Japanese, who treated them as dispensable animals.

On the Perez ranch only Mama Pai, Da, Carmen and Joseph

were left to work there. Papa and the others helped when they were able to return home in the evening, but since the Americans began bombing in the middle of June, they rarely returned home. When Mariquita had first gone to Tå'i in March, she was assigned to help

Japanese agricultural camp. (M.A.R.C. Photo Collection)

prepare food to be cooked and trucked to the various campsites. Later, she was assigned to a labor gang to do agricultural fieldwork near Manenggon, a farming area to the south. There she toiled in the hot sun from sunrise to sunset with very little rest and a meager ration of food. While there, she often witnessed the mistreatment of her helpless co-laborers, herself an occasional victim. But now she had a new assignment, and it would be the final test of her strength.

Tå'i was the headquarters of the *Kaikontai* and when several high-ranking officers arrived there at the end of June, girls considered desirable were selected to work as their personal servants. Mariquita was one of those selected, and she was forced to return to Tå'i.

The main camp of the *Kaikontai* consisted of three makeshift dwellings for the officers. In the center of the camp was a large mango tree, its shading limbs sometimes providing a brief respite from the difficulties that faced the twelve young women who had been ordered to work there. For those modest young women, whose backgrounds never prepared them for such servitude, it was a horrifying experience from which they would never recover.

Besides cooking, laundering and the general cleaning of the officers' quarters, they were compelled to serve their masters, including bathing and massaging them. If they refused, they were beaten. Their servitude extended to the cutting of the officers' toenails, and under the threat of death, some were forced to submit to other desires.

From the first day she worked for the Japanese officers, Mariquita had difficulty concealing her resentment, but she controlled her feelings with silence and did the work expected of her. She suspected that there would come a time when one of the officers would try to force her to sleep with him and she decided that if the situation arose, she would rather die than disgrace her husband and lose her dignity.

The girls who were there were isolated from the other Guamanians who worked at the camp and were not allowed to converse with one another. And, if for any reason one of the officers was displeased, all the girls were punished. This rule was made evident the first morning when the girls were lined up for inspection. One of their requirements was to be neat and clean. That day one of the girls wore a soiled dress. All the girls were slapped, the offender harshly struck with a stick, and those who made any noise or cried were likewise hit.

Mariquita felt sorry for the other girls, some of whom she knew, especially those younger than herself who had never before left their family. She was frightened but outwardly she tried to set an example of courage. In days to come, she often volunteered to bathe and massage an officer to spare a young girl from being humiliated. This compassionate gesture helped to single her out from the other girls, as did her appearance, and she caught the attention of the commanding officer, the head *taicho*.

The first two weeks had tested Mariquita's determination to bear the unpleasantness of the situation. At least she had been able to return home several times, sometimes in the comforting presence of Frankie, carrying food she had stolen from the camp, food she made sure did not include parts of the dogs she had seen butchered and skinned.

Upon her return, she would laugh and play with her children and smother them with her love, and at night, she would whisper her fears to her mother.

On her last visit, she told her mother of her decision that she would rather die than disgrace her husband by sleeping with the

Japanese. Alarmed, Mama Pai had responded, "Tita, I want you alive, not dead. You have to do what you must to stay alive. You have no choice! I will take the responsibility, and I will be the one to answer to Eddie. Tita, he will understand. Do not do anything foolish, my dear daughter."

"Mama, I could never do that," Mariquita had said. "Eddie is the only one who will ever touch me."

"And Chris and Helen, what of them? Have you thought of them?"

"If I could not respect myself, I could never face my children, Mama."

"You do not realize the seriousness of what you are saying," Mama Pai said firmly. "Tita, I am older and wiser than you, maybe not in all things, but I am in life. I know that time will heal your wounds. You are only talking this way because of the cruel things that are happening to you and you are confused. Do what you must to stay alive, if not for me, then for Eddie and the children. And know Tita, I will always be with you."

Mama Pai continued her argument. She knew that Mariquita was listening, but she was also aware that her daughter had already made up her mind. She pleaded with Mariquita, she cried, they both cried, and they prayed, but in the end their positions remained unchanged.

After that visit everything seemed to be happening at once. The Americans started bombing again. Uncle Pepe was suspected of aiding an American serviceman still in hiding and was savagely beaten. Family members were scattered and there were reports of many atrocities being committed by the frantic Japanese.

As the bombings intensified, Mariquita was confined to the camp. Under difficult conditions, she did what she was told to the best of her ability. At night, she slept in a dugout shelter with the other girls, and she was scared.

The head *taicho* was a tough, seasoned soldier of war. He was tall, thin and dark, with a scarred face and a wispy gray beard. He was sometimes referred to as *Batbudu*, bearded.

As the commanding officer, an authoritative position he relished, he was ruthless, and there was no question that women should be servile.

Mariquita had first gained his attention by her physical charm, her grooming and femininity. He delighted in having her do his bidding. Frequently, he asked the Japanese interpreter in charge of the girls to send her to be his handmaiden. What captured his attention was her apparent willingness to serve him, and soon the other officers knew that she was reserved for him. He did not know that Mariquita's passivity was only the result of the acceptance of her fate in order to protect herself and the other girls.

There was something, however, that disturbed the *taicho*. No matter what she was doing, she appeared detached, indifferent to his existence. Just to work for him was not all he wanted from her. She was there to please him and he desired her.

Each day, the *taicho* tried to impress upon her that he was not only the commanding officer of the camp, but her master. And each day she disturbed him more by ignoring him.

He began to slap her for mistakes, real or invented, and to forcefully demonstrate his power over her. Her bow was not correct. She did not serve his food properly. She forgot to say *san* (Mr.) after *taicho* when addressing him. And she was happy about the American planes. But since Mariquita was conscientious about everything she did in the presence of the *taicho*, she knew the real reason for the criticisms and reprimands: he wanted her.

There were many things the *taicho* would do, but he would not physically force a girl to have sex with him as some of the other soldiers did. He was an officer and from a distinguished family, reared with a strict sense of honor, and he would not dishonor himself in this respect. Also, he had never had to; those in his past had willingly accepted his advances because of his position. He wanted Mariquita to submit willingly to his superiority, and sex would be the ultimate proof of this submission.

From the beginning she had repulsed every sexual move he had made toward her. At first, he had only shown displeasure, but soon he had begun to slap her, and now with his anger mounting, she expected the brutal slaps she received and stood still for them. The *taicho* did not know Mariquita. With each offensive act, destined to make her relent, her determination to die rather than accept his sexual advances was strengthened. What she did not know was that part of his rage was due to the recent success of the American forces in the Pacific.

As the days passed, he sensed that she would not yield. Her scorn infuriated him and every day, with each touch of her unfeeling hands as she massaged him, he became angrier.

He was also plagued with the thought that he was losing face with his fellow officers and had lowered himself by making her so important.

He began making her life more miserable. While the Americans were bombing and shelling the island in earnest, he felt his position further weakened and he thought he detected a look of challenge in her eyes. The battle of wills continued and as the bombardment by the Americans increased, so did his passion.

He slowly began to make her life unbearable. He would have all the girls slapped, hit and kicked for anything she did to upset him. Mariquita, who so wanted to help them, was now the cause of some of their pain.

The other girls had their own struggles to cope with and each would bear some scar or ache in the future as a reminder. For the time being, they were managing to survive, and they could do nothing to help Mariquita.

The *taicho* began to hate this girl, Mariquita, whom he knew was married to an American prisoner of war in Japan and was now waiting for the Americans to return. In desperation, he challenged her with force and she violently pushed him away. He hit her, knocking her down. Oh how he hated this "disrespectful dog," as he called her. She would pay for saying no to a Japanese officer in the Imperial Japanese

Army! He called the Japanese interpreter and ordered him to tie her to the lime tree next to the hut and beat her with a bamboo stick. "Ha! At last she is crying," he gloated. "She is calling her mother."

The next day he had her tied again to the tree, this time denying her food and water. She wept. She cried for her mother. She could see the horror in the faces of the girls as they moved by. To one she said, "Don't give me water or they will kill us both." At least she had the satisfaction that the *taicho* never wanted her to serve him again. Mariquita's faith, her children, and the hope of Eddie's return kept her from succumbing to the many outrages.

Between the punishments, Mariquita moved about the camp in a state of terror, frightened for her life. She had thought of running away, but surely, she would have been killed when caught. And what would happen to the other girls if she attempted such a foolish thing? She prayed continuously, asking God to forgive her for anything she may have done wrong in her life and she asked for His help.

11
Death and Liberation

THE AMERICANS POUNDED THE island day and night with explosives, and in retaliation, the Japanese turned on the Guamanian people. On July 12, 1944, Father Duenas was one of several people beheaded in Tå'i by the *Kaikontai* after suffering weeks of torture. Many others were beaten, tortured and killed elsewhere – some were herded into caves and killed with grenades.

In the midst of this inferno, Mariquita and the other girls awaited their fate. Periodically, bombs and shells exploded in the camp area, but the girls were punished if they ran and hid. However, preferring punishment to probable death, they often did, seeking protection in the dugout shelter where they slept and kept their belongings. Between bombardments, in addition to their other duties, the girls were now required to

Invasion forces (top). Rubble from the bombardment of Guam at the end of the war (bottom). (M.A.R.C. Photo Collection)

take care of the Japanese wounded brought to the camp. Some of those seriously injured remained in the camp, and of those assigned to Mariquita, the one with the stinking, rotted arm always tested her ability to overcome nausea. During this time, a day did not pass without some form of cruel punishment imposed upon the girls, anything that would help release the Japanese officers' frustrations. The girls were even accused of starting the morning cook fire to signal American planes, when in reality it had been the first chore demanded of them each day.

Fearful she might do something wrong, Mariquita remained constantly alert and slept very little. It helped that she was not continuously under the watchful eye of the commanding officer, but it mattered less now as all the Japanese appeared to be in a state of madness and anyone in their proximity was a potential victim of their rage.

Standing under the now damaged mango tree to protect her from the rain, Mariquita shook as another bomb exploded nearby. She did not know that her family and precious children had passed under guard through Tå'i the night before with hundreds of other Guamanians on their way south where they were struggling to survive at a concentration camp unfit for human beings. They had been ordered to go there by the Japanese, who wanted the Guamanians away from their encampments and under their complete control. After two-and-a-half years of occupation, they were convinced that when the Americans invaded, the Guamanians would aid them. Before another bomb exploded, she ran to the dugout.

Several days later, Mariquita learned of the family's move to Manenggon from a girl in the camp who had received a message from one of the cook's helpers. Besides the hopelessness of her situation, Mariquita now had to contend with the thought of the heightened danger to her family and she began to break. Then suddenly most of the Guamanians in Tå'i were ordered to leave for Manenggon, and by some miracle, Mariquita was one of those ordered to go. With a ray of hope she joined a large group of men, women, boys and girls leaving late that night in the pouring rain, prodded by guards who harassed them every step of the way. They reached their destination by daybreak.

When they arrived in Manenggon it was still raining and many were sick from the night march. The ragged assembly was herded into a large guardhouse overlooking the Manenggon valley. On the outside of the guardhouse were mounted machine guns that were trained on the hundreds of primitive shelters, mired in mud, that the Guamanians had built.

An officer began to call out the names of those who would be returning to Tå'i. Mariquita survived the list, but before she could savor the happiness of not having to return, one of the girls was taken off the list, and she heard her name, "Maria Perez Howard" called to replace her. The *taicho* had ordered the American wife to return!

Perhaps as a last act of kindness, the Japanese allowed those who were to return to Tå'i a little bit of time to contact relatives in the camp. With difficulty, and in the company of two armed guards, Mariquita found her family's palm thatched lean-to. On hearing Mama Pai answer her inquiry as to who lived there, Mariquita's eyes filled with tears.

Mama Pai came to the opening and was taken aback at the sight of her daughter. Before her stood Mariquita, disheveled, wet and dirty, looking like a frightened animal with two dangerous guards at her side. Mama Pai quickly went to her daughter and took her in her arms, only to have the guards abruptly pull Mariquita back.

In Chamorro, Mariquita whispered, "Where are my children Mama?"

"They are here with me and are asleep, my little girl."

"Do not wake them. And the others, are they here?"

"The older ones are gone, but Papa and the others are inside. And you, Tita, what about you?"

"I am returning to Tå'i. I may not come back. Take good care of my babies, Mama, for I shall die before I do anything to make me ashamed to face my husband."

Mariquita then turned and left, leaving her mother weeping at the entrance to the hut.

She was half-dragged to a waiting car as her legs could barely support her. The sadness she felt was as great as when Eddie had left, and she could hardly control her tears.

A friend who had been with her in Tå'i was in the car and had also been ordered to return. They were joined by Conception Torre, a nurse.

The three girls sobbed in the back seat of the car as the driver spun away from the camp. Shaking, Mariquita kept repeating between sobs, "Please let's say a prayer, let's say a prayer," more to herself than to those beside her.

"Our Father, who ... who art in heaven, hallowed be thy name. Thy kingdom come ... thy will be done on earth as it is in heaven."

The head *taicho* emerged from his quarters when the car carrying Mariquita arrived. He sneered when he saw her, stood a moment watching, then retreated inside. For several days, Mariquita only saw him from a distance and each time she shook uncontrollably with fear.

Incessant bombing added to her predicament at the camp as it filled with wounded and half-crazed soldiers. There was barely enough food to feed those within the camp, let alone those who were arriving from the outlying districts. The camp became a center of confusion, and surrounding it were broken and smoldering trees. Despite it all, the girls were required to continue their service.

As she had done everyday since the end of June, except for that one morning in Manenggon, Mariquita lined up for inspection at daybreak on the morning of July 18, 1944, three days before the beginning of the liberation of her people, and six days before her twenty-fourth birthday. Making an unusual appearance, the head *taicho* was there for the inspection. He accused some of the girls of being late. Mariquita was one of them. The girls were beaten with a wooden stick and slapped. Mariquita was beaten more severely than the rest. Being small and weak from the events of the past weeks, she winced under the blows, and as a result, she was beaten harder. The *taicho* took out his sword in anger and struck her with the blunt edge. He scolded and cursed her. Her head began bleeding profusely. The others were then told to go back to work, and Mariquita was ordered to go to the *taicho*'s quarters and wait there for him.

Mariquita remained in the *taicho*'s quarters until late that evening when a Japanese official inquired whether the *taicho* had finished his investigation of her. His answer was affirmative and the official led her away toward the woods. Mariquita was never seen again.

Anigua Civilian Refugee Camp
November 26, 1944

My Dear Mrs. Levada Howard,

The letter which you sent to Guam addressed to Mrs. Mariquita Howard through Mayor Teller Ammons, U.S.M.C. was read to me by the Mayor on September 30, 1944 and found Chris and Helen, your two paternal grandchildren in the best state of health. The two children, my family, and I all hope you and Mr. Howard the same.

Chris Howard was born September 17, 1940 and is now a fine and lovely boy. Helen Howard was born November 29, 1941 and is also a fine and lovely girl. They speak English and think of their dear father, you, and Mr. Howard a lot. They'd like to see you and long to go to the United States to see you.

My family and I have been taking care of the two young Howards to the best of our ability. We still live in the Camp and are all well and fine.

My son-in-law [Edward] Neal Howard W.T.2C. U.S. Navy is in Japan. We have always been praying that he will come back to Guam to see his two little children and us again.

As for Mrs. Mariquita Howard, your daughter-in-law and daughter of mine, I regret very much to inform you that she is not with us now. During the latter part of the Japanese Occupation of Guam, all men and women were forced to work for the Japanese agricultural activities on the island. Mrs. Howard was forced to work and assigned to do household work for agricultural officials in our ranch district of Sinajana and was only allowed to visit us there twice a week.

On July 12, 1944 we were sent to the concentration camp of Manenggon in Yona. Mrs. Howard was not sent with us. She visited us there two times … it is with our greatest regret to inform you that since her last visit we have not heard of her or her whereabouts to this day.

Chris and Helen send best regards to you and Mr. Howard. I will now close and hope to hear from you soon.

Your Friend,
Josefa Aguon Perez

My Dear Mrs. Howard,

Received your letter with best health of the children and us. Based on the rumors I've heard about Mariquita, our wishes for her living are hopeless. I am very sorry that Mariquita had to die this horrible way, but praises from lots of people about her has gotten into my ears.

Her story, which I've heard, was like this. Since the beginning of her job, she was called upon by the officer of that activity to come and sit upon his lap. Mariquita answered angrily, "I can not do that. I'm married and I've got a husband!" The officer then asked, "Who is your husband?" Mariquita replied that he was an American in the Navy now a prisoner in Japan. Knowing this, he from that time hated her and would slap her. One week later, the officer returning from his job again called upon Mariquita to come to him. Since she refuses, immediately the officer of the day gives the officer his sword and he struck her with its back. Mariquita's head was bleeding … the officer called one of his Army boys and told him to finish her in the woods. Minutes later, the Army boy returned and told [him] that the job is done, as all the girls could know by the signs of the sweating messenger.

Praying that Eddie will return home safely and may God protect him. The children call their father, Daddy. Every time they open a magazine and happen to see a picture of a man and a girl they would say that they are their parents who had gone on a picnic.

Sending you the children will be a good thing, as their mother had wanted for them to go and live a life of happiness and much education.

Buying the children's needs here is very hard since there are only a few things of which they need that are sold here. You need not send us money because I have a little money on hand. My husband is still in the Navy and my two sons are working. My four other children are still attending school ... I knew it would be better for them to continue their schooling.

Chris received one pair of pants and a shirt from the Red Cross. Helen received two dresses from Colonel Archibald. If you received a picture of the children, you'll see that Chris has a bandage on his feet, which I put on myself as a sign of having a sore foot, which was the real excuse for Chris not having any shoes. Chris would like to have a chicken ready for him when he arrives there. Helen would like to have some dolly ready, too. They are so anxious to go there as I told them that they will have lots of happiness in the ranch. He likes to raise chickens.

He has one small chicken here and he even let the chicken sleep with him. Helen likes to be the mother, because she has one small teddy bear here and every now and then she will spank it for not going to sleep.

Lots of kisses and hugs from them. May you always be in happiness and God bless you two. Best regards from all in the family.

Sincerest Regards,
Josefa Perez

Josefa with Helen and Chris, whose foot is bandaged as mentioned in Josefa's letter. (Josephine "Joey" San Agustin Photo Collection)

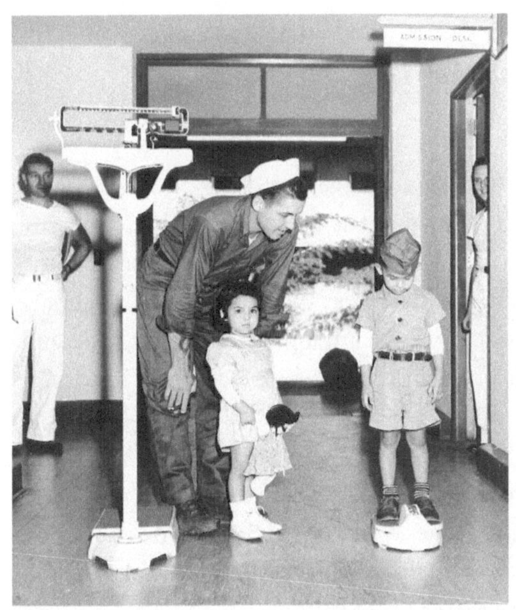

Edward, Chris and Helen
at Aiea Heights Naval Hospital
in Hawaii in October 1945,
shortly after they were reunited.
(Perez Howard Photo Collection)

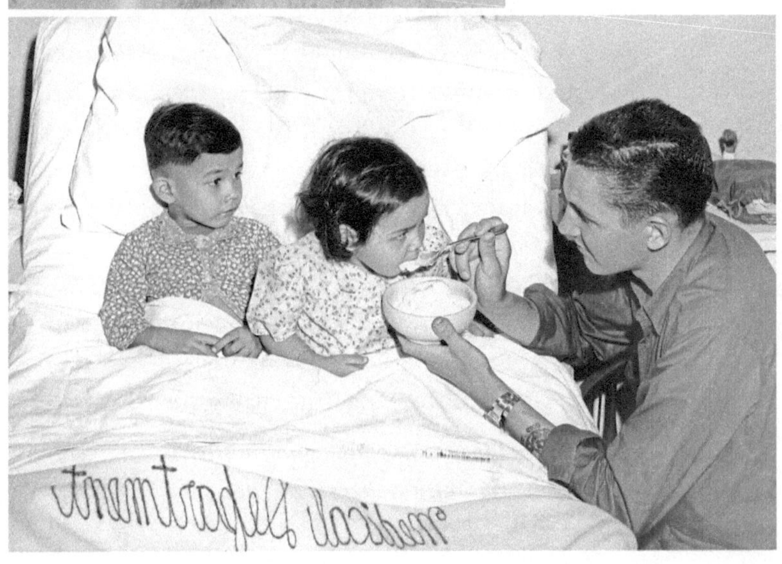

Epilogue

MY MOTHER WAS NEVER seen again and her body was never found, although a thorough search was conducted by my family and American troops. In September 1945, over a year after the Americans had retaken Guam and after the surrender of Japan, my father returned to the island. He also attempted to find her body, and although he was able to locate the approximate location of her death, he could not find her remains.

My father endured those years as a prisoner of war in Japan with the hope of someday returning to the waiting arms of Mariquita. It never occurred to him that she would not be there. The shock and grief he experienced on his return, coupled with his POW experience, would haunt him for the rest of his life.

This year, Guam will be celebrating the 75th anniversary of the liberation by American forces from the cruel Japanese occupation of Guam during World War II. While it is a celebration of being liberated from war, it is also a remembrance of a people who withstood numerous violations against them, including personal remembrances of this tragic period in Guam's history.

Lest we forget, here is an excerpt from *The Long, and the Short, and the Tall*, a book by American soldier Alvin Josephy, written shortly after the war. I read this book during my research on the retaking of Guam. Under the heading "The Chamorros," he wrote:

> *The jungle was very thick. It was quiet and ghostly. And it might have been my imagination, but there was a bad smell in the air.*

Suddenly we came to a clearing. There, spread out on the ground, were about forty bodies of young men. They had their legs drawn up against their chests and had their arms tied behind their backs. They lay in awkward positions - on their sides and their stomachs, and on their knees - like swollen, purple lumps. And none of them had heads, they had all been decapitated. The heads lay like bowling balls all over the place.

There was a truck nearby with more bodies and lopped-off heads in it. It looked as if the Japanese had been loading all the bodies and heads in the truck, but had been frightened away and had left everything behind.

At first, …we thought they were Japanese soldiers, killed by their own men in some sort of harakiri business. But then, by the clothes, we knew they were young Chamorran men. There was one beheaded woman in the truck.

Before the bodies were buried, many of us visited the frightful scene and saw the victims of the Japanese atrocity. A Guamanian youth told us they were men who had been taken from the concentration camps, charged with being American spies.

When I read this, I cried, thinking that the woman may have been my mother. But, after talking again with the women who were with her the day of her death, they said it was not her as she was in Tå'i and the clothes the woman had on were not any Mariquita had with her. I believe them.

Although the odds were against us, Helen and I and the rest of the family survived the war. We survived physically, but like everyone else who endured the harsh occupation, we have been mentally affected by what had transpired.

Shortly after Guam was retaken, my grandmother Perez and grandmother Howard were able to contact one another through the military command and the American Red Cross. After my father arrived on island, it was then decided that Helen and I would go with him to Indiana.

My father remained in the U.S. Navy for twenty years and retired as a warrant officer. Shortly after his retirement, he entered Indiana University where he graduated with the highest honors and obtained a Master's degree. In 1981, he retired again, this time as director of the Vigo County Library in Terre Haute, Indiana. Afterwards he went to live in Carlisle, Indiana, not far from his birthplace, with his wife Betty Jo. I was with him when he died on March 25, 1990, at the Richard L. Roudebush VA Medical Center in Indianapolis.

While in the Navy, one of his tours of duty was a two-year stay on Guam from 1949-1951. At that time, my sister and I were reunited with our Guam family. Our immediate family then included our dear step-mother Jean, who died in 1963 and her two children, Charles and Barbara.

During our stay, my love for my Guam family grew and I can truthfully say that those years were the happiest years of my childhood. I held this time close to my heart and finally returned to Guam in November 1979.

There was a time, shortly after my return, when I thought that maybe my mother had survived and just didn't remember who she was and was taken in by another family. But that was just wishful thinking. I wondered what my life would have been like if she had not been killed and my father had not been a prisoner of war. I also wondered what Guam would have looked like, particularly the city of Agana, if it had not been the subject of massive and prolonged American bombardment. As for me, would I have become a priest like my mother wanted? A lot of thoughts came to mind.

In every Chamorro family there are stories similar to those of my family, and many of these stories are only now being heard. All of us who were in Guam during the war were victims, but to some extent, I was one of the lucky ones; I was young enough to not remember the reality of it. In the war between the United States and Japan, Guam was the loser.

As I became more settled on Guam, I also became more unsettled concerning my identity. I was Chamorro but I was also a stateside American. I didn't identify fully with either nor could I reconcile the two. By my second year on the island, I had settled somewhat amicably in my new environment finding it easier to accept what was, and not question what wasn't. But as time passed and I met more relatives and family friends, I was forced to leave the comfort of superficiality. I became acutely aware of my shortcomings and began to suffer embarrassment. Not only did I not speak the language, I had little knowledge of the island, its history and culture. Above all else, I could not remember my mother, through whose identity I called myself Chamorro.

All I knew of my mother was from the few photographs I had of her and from what people had told me. My father never talked about her. Frankly, I hadn't wanted to know anything more because I knew she had been killed by the Japanese and I didn't want to dwell on it. I am one of those who shy away from unpleasantries and what could be more unpleasant than to think of the death of one's own mother? Now that I was living on Guam, however, among relatives and friends who knew her, I could not continue to leave her in the past. After a time, I got used to hearing about her and speaking about her. In time, I actually began to use her as a crutch to shore up my own lack of identity. The more I used her identity, however, the more I needed to know about her and soon I was asking questions and delving into the history of Guam, particularly the war years.

While navigating this self-identity problem, I applied for and received a grant from the Insular Arts Council to do research and write *Mariquita*. This identity problem, at times, was reflected in the story. Another dilemma I had was keeping the story focused on Mariquita, as my father's story was not only entwined but equally strong. In addition, I had to keep my own feelings at bay while I was writing, particularly after my father sent me some documents relating to her death.

During the writing of the book, I grew to love my mother, and toward the end of this difficult undertaking, I discovered that I had an emotional memory of her. At the beginning, it was easy to write about her because I was writing about someone I didn't know, but as I got deeper into her story, it became increasingly difficult for me to keep my emotions intact. One night, after finishing a writing stint, I was heating up something to eat when I started an argument with my roommate. All of a sudden, I became angry, picked up the food-laden frying pan and hurled it to the floor. And then I burst into tears. All of the emotions I had kept pent up simply exploded. The person I was writing about was my mother! The enormity of the emotional revelation had unplugged a torrent of buried pain. I may not have remembered her in the ordinary sense, but I had a deeply rooted memory of her and I was remined that day about how much I loved her and missed her.

In gathering information for my book, I learned that Japan had not paid war reparations to the people of Guam. I also became highly sensitive to the many atrocities committed during the occupation, and when I learned that Japanese "defense" ships were visiting Guam and were at Naval Station, I deeply resented their being here and picketed the ships with a sign reading, "War Reparations for Guam."

It was during this period of time that I met Senator Cecilia Bamba and began to voluntarily work with her on the issue of war reparations. War reparations are the compensation by a nation defeated in war for economic losses suffered by the victor or for crimes committed against individuals, payable in money, labor, goods, etc. Because Chamorros were U.S. nationals at the time of the war, it was the United States' responsibility of the U.S. to obtain war reparations for them from Japan. Instead, the U.S. signed the Treaty of Peace with Japan and committed to paying for all wartime claims made against Japan by U.S. citizens and nationals.

The issue of war reparations was the first of a number of Chamorro concerns which raised my consciousness as a Chamorro and in turn lead me to begin questioning the United States. I learned how for over 350 years, Guam has been colonized by Spain, Japan, and the United States. It's people have been treated at best like second-class citizens. As Guam's administering power, the United States added Guam to the United Nations' list of the world's non-self-governing territories in 1946. And in their first report to the United Nations, stated that the people of Guam were called Chamorro.

Shortly after Senator Bamba left office, she became the executive director of the Commission on Self-Determination and I applied for and became her administrative assistant. It was during the course of my time as administrative assistant that I came to terms with my identity. When the issue of limiting the vote to only the Chamorro people in the self-determination plebiscite surfaced, I was faced with the question of whether my right to vote was because I was an American or because I was Chamorro. Should I go against "limiting" the vote or should I embrace it?

Researching the issue, I learned that self-determination was the right of a colonized people to decide their own political status and form of government, without outside influence. I learned that, in this case, "people" meant "all persons of a racial, national, religious or linguistic group, or group of persons with common traditional, historical, or cultural ties". I learned that whether or not one lived on Guam, U.S. citizens who were not Chamorro did not have the right to partake in Guam's decolonization vote, because they were not colonized. Self-Determination belonged to the Chamorro people alone, as it is a right that was taken away distinctly from them, a right which transcends their status as U.S. citizens.

Yes, I was both an American and a Chamorro. But I was an American through citizenship and a Chamorro through birth. In understanding this difference, I began to know myself. Now, looking back, I wonder how something so simple could have remained hidden from me for so long. I had actually seen my being American in much the same way as I now see myself as a Chamorro. I saw my being an American as a member of an ethnic group. But I believe that being Chamorro by birth is not, in its self, enough, it really has to be in one's heart.

During the height of the controversy over who should be allowed to vote in the self-determination plebiscite, a number of us came together with the belief that only the Chamorro people had that right to self-determination, and we subsequently founded the Organization of People for Indigenous Rights (OPI-R). This organization, of which I was a member, aside from self-determination, also addressed other issues, such as: war reparations, land rights, historical preservation, and immigration. We also supported the anti-nuclear issue and issues of other indigenous peoples.

In closing, I guess one could say that my Chamorro activism began with my mother. I think she would be proud of me for my activism. In writing this book, it was not her face that I recalled, but her warmth and motherly love. Looking at my life, it appears that the hardships I have had to face and overcome prepared me to write this book so that my mother and others who suffered the occupation would be remembered. It is written with the hope that people will know through the life of one girl, the sad history of the occupation of Guam.

Appendix

LC-4-1   WPK/jk   5 May 1947
MEMORANDUM
To: Officer-in Charge, Claims Division
Subj: HOWARD, Maria Perez, death of

Herewith is a verbatim summary of testimony taken by the previous Land and Claims Commission and contained in the file on the above subject.

2 October 1945

Eddie Bordallo was today questioned regarding the death of Maria Perez Howard. He stated:

1. He was working at a Jap Agricultural Camp. In early July 1944 he saw her there. She was working for the Japanese Navy Officer in charge of the Agricultural Camp, as a housemaid. She appeared to be in good health. He then went away to concentration camp and did not see her again.

2. On 31, July 1944 he was going with a 77th Division Army patrol as a guide and they found a dead body of a woman, at the place where the Jap Agricultural Camp had been located. Body was decomposed and the face was unrecognizable. The woman had been wearing a light blue dress. This was the only body they found at this place which was located in Price District in Tae [sic].

5 October 1945

Lorraine Bordallo was today questioned regarding Maria Perez Howard. She stated:

1. She and Maria were living in Manenggon when one morning Japs called out the girls and told the girls that they were to work at a certain camp. It was the Japanese Agricultural Camp Headquarters near Pago at Tae [sic]. This was early in July 1944. After they had been there about three weeks, one morning the cook told the Jap officials that some of the girls had been coming to work late and named Maria as one of them. Previous to this Maria had apparently been particularly suspected and disliked by the Japs, apparently because she was the wife of an American serviceman. Also it was rumored that she refused to sleep with the Japs, particularly a certain Japanese leader. The girls who were reported late including Maria were beaten with a stick of wood and slapped. Maria was beaten more severely than the rest. She was smaller and not as strong and winced under the blows, and as a result she was beaten harder and finally the Jap leader took out his sword and hit her head with the blunt edge. The Jap appeared to be scolding her at the time. Her head started bleeding. The others were then told to go back to work, and Maria was told to go to the Jap leader's quarters and wait there for him. From then on other girls including Lorraine did not see her. At 10:00 p.m. one of the girls who was working in the Jap officer's quarters told the other girls that Mariquita had disappeared. That was the last time she was ever seen.

2. About two or three days later Lorraine and all the other girls left Tae [sic] to go back to the concentration camp at Manenggon. Maria was not with them. The Japs had left one day earlier, and the girls were the last ones to leave the camp at Tae. They left under the supervision of a Saipanese.

3. Lorraine expressed the opinion that if a body of a girl was found at that camp in Tae [sic] several days afterwards it was

undoubtedly the body of Maria because there was nobody in that vicinity it could be.

Maria Cruz Borja (Paulino) was today questioned as to possible information she might have in the case of Maria Perez Howard. She stated:

1. She was one of the girls, together with Lorraine Bordallo and Maria, who were taken from Manenggon to Tae [sic] to work at the Jap Agricultural Camp for the officers.

2. She was one of the ones beaten with Maria on the morning of Maria's disappearance.

3. She saw Maria Howard at 9:00 p.m. that evening, leaving the Jap leader's quarters where she had apparently remained since that morning when she was ordered there after being beaten. An official had inquired whether the Jap leader had finished investigating her and when the answer was affirmative he had led her away towards the woods. She never saw Maria again.

4. Maria Howard was wearing and had worn that day a rust colored dress made of a brightly colored Japanese silken material which she Maria Borja had loaned. She is sure of this because she remembers trying to call Maria Howard's attention before inspection that morning to the fact it was dirty, so she could clean it up before inspection.

5. The circumstances under which Maria was last seen by her were typical of those under which people whom the Japs have decided to kill had been led away in the past.

J.E.M.
William P. Katsirubas
Investigator

Acknowledgements

I T IS IMPOSSIBLE TO name all who helped and encouraged me in the writing of this book. Please know that those who are not listed here are equally appreciated and are not forgotten.

I extend my sincere gratitude to the following: The Juan Taijeron and Josefa Aguon Perez family; Regina C. Reyes Acosta; Frank Agualo; Katherine Aguon; Cecilia C. Bamba; Rosalia Torres Baza; Magdalena Bayani (Santos San Nicolas); Monsignor Oscar Calvo; Ray Castro; Lyle W. Eads; Maria C. Borja Efe; Maria Perez Buffery; Beatrice Emsley; Maria C. Flores (San Nicolas Cruz); BJ Howard; Anthony Iannarelli; William B. Lloyd; Rosalina Crisostomo Mabesa; Jaoquin Manibusan; Rosa Payne Murer; Lourdes Murphy; Darlene Norman; Donna Oliver; Kathleen Owings; Greg and Eca Sablan; Agnes Mateo Salas; Concepcion Slotnick (Torre); Pedro Sanchez; Margarita Torre; and John Zahnen.

I give special thanks to my father, Edward Neal Howard, my aunt, Carmen Aguon Perez, Marian Johnston Taitano, and Lourdes M. Perez.

Additionally, I would also like to thank the staff of the Micronesian Area Research Center, the staff of the Nieves Flores Memorial Library, and the Vigo County Library, Terre Haute, Indiana

The initial writing for this project was aided by the support of the Insular Arts Council, Office of the Governor and was funded by an appropriation from the 15th Guam Legislature through grants from the National Endowment for the Arts.

For this edition, I sincerely thank my editor, Victoria-Lola Leon Guerrero for her insight and expertise, and the staff of UOG Press.

Without the support and help from my friend, Adelaide E. Bouchet, this book may not have been written.

About the Author

Chris Perez Howard believes that his adventurous spirit and endless curiosity are responsible for his unconventional life. Among his experiences, he served in the U.S. military; worked for the American Express Co. in New York; struggled as an artist in Rome, Italy; lived in Yap, the Seychelles, and the Philippines; and went to Africa to see wild animals in their natural habitat.

In Guam, he has worked as a teacher, a news editor for the *Guam Tribune*, an assistant to the president of the Guam Community College, and a press secretary for the Governor of Guam.

Academically, he attended the University of Alabama and Indiana University, and he graduated magna cum laude from the University of New Hampshire with a bachelor of fine arts degree.

Chris is also a CHamoru rights activist, and is a former chairman of the Organization of People for Indigenous Rights (OPI-R) and has presented testimony before the United Nations and the U.S Congress.

Presently, he is working on his novel – *I Mestisan Engles.*

www.ingramcontent.com/pod-product-compliance
Lightning Source LLC
Chambersburg PA
CBHW061453210726
48287CB00007B/2486